Mills &

A chance to read and collect some of the best-loved novels from Mills & Boon – the world's largest publisher of romantic fiction.

Every month, four titles by favourite Mills & Boon authors will be re-published in the *Classics* series.

A list of other titles in the *Classics* series can be found at the end of this book.

Lilian Peake

THE REAL THING

MILLS & BOON LIMITED
LONDON · TORONTO

First published 1972
Australian copyright 1980
Philippine copyright 1980
This edition 1980

ISBN 0 263 73376 9

Set in 10/11 pt. Linotype Plantin

Made and printed in Great Britain by Richard Clay (The Chaucer Press) Ltd, Bungay, Suffolk

CHAPTER I

It was the sort of weather, Cleone decided, that brought out the best in you. Even the birdsong was more intense than usual, as if the birds themselves felt the need to respond frantically to the day's perfection, before the climate reverted to its inevitable English greyness.

The sky, empty of cloud, was a Mediterranean blue, but the countryside was English to the core—green fields, hedgerows, red-roofed cottages and the hills beyond. Cleone felt a reciprocity, a give-and-take ebb and flow between her and the country around her, and knew that if she ever had to leave it she would be only half alive.

Her arm was pressed closely to her side, holding firmly in place the reporter's notebook which was one of the tools of her trade. She was a journalist, a young and eager member of the reporting staff of the local newspaper, and she was on her way to interview an old lady.

The first time she had called on her, about two weeks before, she had not been well enough to talk to her. 'Come again, my dear,' she had said, 'when I've thrown off this awful cold. I should like to talk to you then.' As she had shown her to the door, the old lady had repeated, as though to extract a promise, 'You will come again, won't you?'

So Cleone was keeping that promise and was going back to hear the old lady's story.

She lifted the heavy black knocker and let it fall gently. There was a long silence, and Cleone began to grow anxious. Was the old lady all right? She was about to knock again, when the latch moved, and the door opened.

'Come in, come in, my dear,' the soft voice invited.

Cleone followed the short, frail figure into the living-room and wondered at such agility in a person of so great an age. The clomp of the walking stick as it hit the woodblock flooring kept perfect time with the quick firm steps, giving Cleone the impression that, if the footsteps ever dared to lag behind, the stick would tap out the impatient message, 'Keep up, keep up!'

Her hostess lowered herself carefully into a high-backed armchair and Cleone noticed how neatly her white hair had been combed, how it was smoothed back into a roll round the thin neck and how a hairpin had worked its way out of place and was hanging precariously over the collar of her jacket.

'May I?' asked Cleone, and without waiting for an answer gently pushed the hairpin back into place with a granddaughterly gesture.

'Was that a pin?' the old lady laughed. 'They're the bane of my life! Sometimes I think they've got minds of their own, they will not obey my old fingers.'

But Cleone knew those 'old fingers' were still capable of producing works of art, and that was the reason for her visit. The old lady was known locally as the 'lace lady', but no one seemed to know for whom her lace was made.

Cleone sat on a stool at the old lady's feet.

'Mrs. Firse is my name, Mrs. Bess Firse,' she said, and waited patiently while it was written down.

Cleone gazed with something approaching awe at the cobweb tracery of loops and flower designs worked into the sample of lace which was put into her hands. She thought it the most beautiful crochet she had ever seen.

'This, my dear, is hairpin crochet and it is done with a hook over a large two-pronged fork. And this,' she held up another specimen of her work, 'is tricot crochet and for this I use a special long hook. You can see what a good fabric it makes.' Mrs. Firse laughed softly. 'When you write your article, say I belong to a world that's gone—a world that liked prettiness and dainty things. You see, my dear,' she went on with a twinkle, 'even the words I use are out of date nowadays!'

'Who do you make this wonderful lace for?' Cleone

asked. 'No one seems to know. Is it for your grandchildren?'

The old lady's face saddened. 'My dear, I'm eighty. My grandson is grown up.' Then she brightened. 'But one day, I hope, he'll give me a great-grandchild.'

'He's married, then?'

She laughed and shook her head. 'But I keep on hoping! He's over thirty now, and I keep telling him—he comes and stays with me sometimes,' she sidetracked, shaking her head. 'I never know when he's coming, he just walks in—I tell him, "You ought to get a young lady." And he says, "I've got half a dozen young ladies." But I say, "Not one you love." And he says, "I love them all, Grandmother!" And then he laughs and says, if it will make me happy, he'll marry the lot!'

Her thin high-pitched laugh invited Cleone to laugh with her and she did. 'And what about you, my dear?' Mrs. Firse asked, dabbing at her eyes which had grown moist with laughter. 'Have you got a young man?'

'I've got Ivor. He works in a bank.'

'And are you going to marry him?'

'I expect so. One day, when we've saved up enough money to get a place of our own.'

'Very sensible,' Mrs. Firse nodded.

They had a cup of tea and talked again. After a while Cleone said she had to go. She left, reminding Mrs. Firse of her promise to make some lace for her soon.

Cleone could have gone back to work by bus, but the sunshine proved too seductive, so she chose the path across the fields instead. She sat down and removed her shoes, and revelled in the sensation of walking over the cool, softly stroking blades of grass. Her sandals swung from her fingers and she carried her notebook in her other hand, and felt she could not ask for more.

She climbed a stile and dropped down into a wooded hollow, putting on her sandals again—twigs and brittle leaves were not as kind to the feet as grass—and looked at the branches above her head. The invitation was too great to resist. She had to indulge that longing to stretch out for a few minutes under her favourite tree.

In the stillness, under the canopy of birdsong and unhampered by the noise of traffic and the smell of petrol fumes, and with only the whisper of the breeze through the leaves to disturb her, she thought about the old lady. She gazed up at the green leaf patterns against the liquid blueness and thought about the delicate lace that worked its way from those wonderful fingers.

She felt in her pocket for the sample Mrs. Firse had given her, drew it out and held up the piece of lace towards the sky. She admired it again, put it away and recalled the pleasant surroundings the old lady lived in, the well-preserved cottage, the good-quality carpets and furniture, and wondered where the money came from to keep her in such comfort.

A bee buzzed round her and stirred her sense of duty. She had to get back or the others would start asking questions. She shook off her torpor and ran the rest of the way. She hurried along the corridor towards the reporters' room, hoping to slip in unnoticed. She would have done if she hadn't felt something stabbing into the sole of her foot. She couldn't walk another step, she decided, without removing the offending object, and took off her sandal, supporting herself on one leg by leaning sideways against the wall.

She tutted as she shook the sandal, muttering, 'It felt like the branch of a tree and it was only a bit of bark!'

'Ah, but is it worse than its bite?'

She turned contemptuously on the speaker. 'If that's supposed to be a joke, Mike, stick to your tea-making. You're better at it.'

A door opened along the corridor, but they ignored it.

'Talking of tea,' the boy went on, 'you missed your cuppa this afternoon. It usually takes a national disaster to make you do that. What happened?'

'I had a cup with an old lady. Much nicer than the stuff you give us.'

'Thanks for the compliment, Cleone which rhymes with peony.' She didn't respond with violence as she usually did when he recited the verse he had made up about her name. Disappointed, he watched her brush the sole of her foot. 'Been going without shoes again? Dirty habit, I call it. Don't let Ivor find out, otherwise he might not marry you!'

This time he got the reaction he wanted. He ducked as a sandal sped through the air. It missed him and was deftly caught by a man standing in the doorway of the editor's office.

'Now you've done it,' Mike hissed. 'That's Mr. Riley's visitor, V.I.P. status, too. Get yourself out of this one!' He wished her luck and went on his way.

The eyes that stared into hers from a distance of about seven feet were brown, quizzical and lazily amused. Then, like twin explorers in search of undiscovered land, they journeyed over her from head to toe, stopping here and there as if for refreshment and rest. They took in the brown wind-ruffled hair, the unflinching hazel eyes, the obstinate cleft in the chin. They looked at her pink open-necked blouse and tightly fitting blue slacks, pausing for a long time at floor level, dwelling first on her sandalled foot, then on her bare one.

The entire action took only a few seconds, but to Cleone, holding her breath, standing on one foot and curling and uncurling her uncovered toes, it seemed like hours.

His eyes, by their slow calculated action, had stripped her clean of all the dignity she possessed and as she walked unevenly towards him, she extended her hand in a pleading gesture. If she had expected him to give her the sandal at once, she was disappointed, because when at last she was standing in front of him, he deliberately put it behind his back. There was nothing for it—she would have to apologise, then perhaps he would take pity on her and hand it over.

She stumbled over the apology and with enough appeal in her eyes to provoke an ancient statue into some sort of response she asked him to return her sandal. But he must have been made of something considerably harder than stone because he did not move a muscle. He remained leaning against the door frame and seemed to be enjoying her slightly abject appearance. At last he spoke.

'Before I hand it over—*if* I hand it over—I should be glad if you would tell me your name.'

With some agitation she looked past him into Mr. Riley's room. It was empty. 'He's not there,' her tormentor informed her. 'He was called away.'

Without giving him the information he had requested, she asked again for her sandal. She was growing anxious. It wasn't that she was afraid of Mr. Riley—he was normally an understanding, tolerant man, but his tolerance might be strained to its limits if he found a member of his reporting staff standing on one foot, pleading with a visitor—a very important visitor—to give her back her shoe, which she had inadvertently thrown at him in the first place.

'Your name?' he requested again, his tone excessively polite.

If telling him her name was the fuse which would light his compassion, then her name he would be told.

'Cleone Aston,' she said, her temper rising. She held out her hand for her property.

A smile flirted with his lips and he looked for a moment very like a dog that had been promised a large, juicy bone. 'Yes, I thought it must be,' he murmured.

The shoe was handed over into fingers that were beginning to stiffen with anger. Having delivered himself of his prize, he stood upright and assumed his V.I.P. posture again. Cleone noted his regular features, his height, his superbly cut suit, his air of supreme self-confidence and self-command. He oozes affluence, Cleone thought, recoiling from him as if afraid of becoming contaminated. Despite his good looks, his brown eyes, now slightly quizzical as he watched her examining him, his well-shaped mouth, now lifted in a half-smile, Cleone did not like him.

'It's not so much him,' she decided, frowning, 'as what goes with him—his background, which fences him in as surely as a double layer of barbed wire, his self-assurance and his maddening ease of manner.' No, she didn't like him at all.

She thanked him, slipped on her sandal and retreated to the reporters' room to write up the old lady's story. She was alone and she was glad. After such an encounter, she needed some time to recover her balance, although she could not understand why. She flicked through her notes and read them again.

'My son,' the old lady had said, 'makes clothes.' Cleone had asked, 'What sort of clothes?' 'Oh,' she had said, 'ladies' things, you know, pretty dresses.'

Cleone had not pursued the subject. After all, it was the old lady she had gone to talk about, not the son.

'Miss Aston,' the editor's head came round the door, 'I've been looking for you. I have a visitor I want you to meet.'

Startled, Cleone stared at him. 'But I don't want to meet your visitor.' She thought the words, opened her mouth to say them, then decided prudently to remain silent. She would have had to give him the reason for her reluctance and that she simply could not do.

'I'll give you a minute to tidy yourself, then just come along, will you?'

That, thought Cleone, was a hint that she needed tidying. She looked in the mirror and supposed she did. She picked a leaf from her hair and combed out the tangles, applied a layer of powder and touched her lips with lipstick. Then she stopped. Why should she bother about the editor's expensive visitor? Anyway, why did Mr. Riley want her to meet him? Was it some sort of pet show and she was one of the exhibits? She felt like a prize-winning poodle when she stood in the editor's room a few minutes later. Mr. Riley's avuncular eyes patted her affectionately and she expected any moment to be told to 'sit'.

His voice was persuasive and his words had the tone of a salesman promoting a product to a reluctant buyer. 'I do believe he's trying to "sell" me,' Cleone thought angrily. If so, then he was up against consumer resistance. The man at the receiving end of the promotions campaign was definitely proving awkward.

After inviting her to sit down, Mr. Riley gave his full attention to his 'customer'. Puzzled, Cleone listened to the editor putting over his sales talk and was surprised at the vigour with which he was pursuing his subject. He was one of the old school of journalists now almost extinct—honest to the point of bluntness, untiring in his pursuit of the truth—'Get your facts right' was his pet phrase, and one on which Cleone declared she had been 'weaned'—an adherent to the old formal style, the stilted language of a few decades ago. If he had not been near retirement, Cleone and her colleagues doubted if he could have survived for much longer in the newspaper jungle.

She came back to the present to find Mr. Riley addressing her.

'Miss Aston, my dear, I'm afraid my enthusiasm in expounding your virtues has carried me away. I omitted to introduce you to my visitor.' He waved them towards each other. 'Miss Aston, Mr. Firse, Mr. Ellis Firse. Miss Aston, as you will have gathered, Mr. Firse, is a valued member of my reporting staff.'

They stood, their eyes met, entangled and broke free and Cleone felt, even as she put her hand briefly in his, that war had been declared.

'We have, I'm sure, met before?' Cleone could have slapped his face for his bland smile. Surely he was not going to tell tales?

He must have seen her sudden anxiety because his smile broadened. 'Your face is surely familiar?'

Taking him literally, Mr. Riley broke into the tight

silence, 'I doubt it, Mr. Firse. A pretty girl like her—a man would remember for certain whether he had met her or not!'

Mr. Firse sat down. 'You're probably right. She must remind me of someone I know. But I could have sworn . . .'

'In your dreams,' Mr. Riley laughed, slapping the table, 'that's where you must have seen her!' Then he became serious. 'But Miss Aston has probably heard of you——'

'Firse Publications?' Cleone interrupted, astonished. 'Publishes magazines——' and she reeled off a string of names.

'My word, Miss Aston,' Mr. Riley said proudly, 'you've done your homework well without any prompting from me.' He turned to his visitor. 'You see what I mean, what I was telling you about her before she came in?'

'I do indeed,' Mr. Firse said gravely.

Cleone looked bewildered. When would Mr. Riley tell her what was going on?

'Mr. Firse has a proposition to make, Miss Aston.' At last we're coming to the point, Cleone thought. 'He has a vacancy—but you tell her, Mr. Firse.'

So Mr. Firse, the lazily tolerant, slightly provocative visitor, became Ellis Firse, the businessman, and told her in clipped, precise tones that, having called in to renew his acquaintance with Mr. Riley—he had met him once at a dinner—he had mentioned his predicament, that he was in search of a young woman journalist with a lively mind and a fresh approach to her work to fill an editorial position which had just become vacant on one of his magazines.

Cautiously and more than a little suspicious, Cleone asked, what sort of editorial position?

It was in a subject, Mr. Firse said expansively, in which, according to his experience, all women regardless of age were interested—fashion.

Cleone recoiled. 'Fashion?' She shook her head. 'Not my line, I'm sorry.'

Mr. Riley gasped. 'But my dear Miss Aston, such an

opportunity——!'

Ellis Firse plainly took offence. He bristled. 'Miss Aston,' he said sharply, 'with a brain as quick and clever as I'm told yours is, I would have thought that nothing would be beyond you.' He sat forward, crossing his legs and pulling the crease in his trousers into a neat, precise line. 'Let's get this clear. I'm offering you the editorship——'

Cleone drew in a short, sharp breath. 'Even more impossible. Out of the question, in fact.'

'I'm offering you the editorship,' he went on as if she had not spoken, 'of a magazine—its name is *Salon*—you might even have heard of it—which deals exclusively with fashion at *haute couture* level. The salary is good,' he named a sum which made her gasp, 'the prospects equally good. By this I mean that we publish a large number of magazines, many of them internationally known, and provided you prove yourself good enough, there should be no barrier to your progress within the company.'

'He's making the carrot really big and juicy,' Cleone thought.

'But,' he went on, 'I'm not going to sell you the job. It surely speaks for itself. If you think you haven't got the necessary ability, intelligence or'—he looked her up and down—'the necessary feeling for that sort of journalism, then'—he shrugged and looked as though he was preparing to leave—'I'm wasting my time.'

She put out her hand. 'Just a minute, Mr. Firse——'

But Mr. Firse rose. Cleone rose, too. 'Mr. Firse, I—I . . .'

'Sit down, both of you,' Mr. Riley pleaded, feeling the situation slipping out of his control. They sat down. He smiled placatingly at his visitor. 'Perhaps, at the back of Miss Aston's mind, is the complete change this would make to her life. You see, Miss Aston is a country girl, aren't you, my dear?'

'You've lived here all your life?' There was doubt now in Ellis Firse's voice.

She nodded.

'I've watched her grow up,' Mr. Riley went on indulgently. 'We've recorded in our paper all her little successes through school and willingly took her on the staff here as a junior reporter. She always had a burning ambition to become a journalist and I knew that anyone as determined as she was must succeed.'

Mr. Firse's doubts seemed to be multiplying. 'So you've never tried your hand at any other sort of journalism?'

'No,' she answered, puzzled by his apparent change of heart, 'but I'm sure I could . . .'

He shook his head. Mr. Riley rushed on, 'She's so domesticated——'

Cleone winced and Ellis Firse smiled. She felt the job sliding out of her grasp. When at first it had seemed hers for the taking, she hadn't wanted it. Now, perversely, when that large juicy carrot was being withdrawn, inch by subtle inch, she felt herself beginning to pant after it and grip it in her teeth before it was whisked out of sight.

Mr. Riley looked anxiously at his watch. Mr. Firse rose and looked at his watch, too. He glanced at Cleone, speculation narrowing his eyes.

'Anyway,' he said, as if bringing the whole discussion to an end, 'the person required for this particular position would need a great many attributes Miss Aston does not seem to possess. Clothes sense,' his eyes flicked over her casual and careless appearance, 'a feeling for fashion, a certain measure of sophistication, feline aggression to use as a defence mechanism against her equally feline contemporaries on other magazines.' He paused. 'I could elaborate, but it's hardly worth my while . . .'

'But Mr. Firse——'

He must have seen the disappointment that was beginning to cloud her eyes because he asked, a little impatiently, 'Yes?'

She blurted out, 'Have you changed your mind completely? Have you withdrawn your offer?'

Taken aback by her bluntness, he seemed to hesitate.

Mr. Riley attempted to act as arbitrator. 'Would it not be better,' he suggested, 'if you both went away somewhere and discussed this by yourselves?' He smiled at Mr. Firse. 'I have little more to add to my eulogies of Miss Aston's character and ability. I can assure you that no matter what would be required of her in such a position, she would undoubtedly be equal to it. I have every confidence in her. What more can I say?'

Ellis Firse considered the matter, then he turned to her with decision. 'Miss Aston, I'm dining at my hotel tonight. If you would care to join me——?' He named the hotel.

Cleone knew she must not hesitate. Somehow, suddenly, she wanted that job, if only to prove to this overbearing individual that she could do it. So she knew she must accept his invitation and be seen to accept with alacrity.

'I should be delighted to dine with you,' she said, with a smile that exuded a confidence which only she knew was false.

Cleone was in the cloakroom combing her hair when she heard Ivor's motorbike slow down and stand throbbing at the kerb, waiting to take her home. Sometimes she was still out on an assignment when he arrived and then he would ride away alone. She lifted her crash helmet from the hook on the wall and as she ran along the corridor, fitted the helmet securely over her head.

Ivor was waiting patiently, as he always did, and they exchanged smiles. They could do little else because the noise of the engine made talking impossible. Cleone settled herself on the seat behind him and held on to his waist. They both looked behind to make sure the road was clear before drawing away from the kerb, and Cleone saw a large, sleek, dark red luxury car pull out to overtake them. The man at the wheel smiled and raised his hand in a lazy, slightly mocking salute, and his very action sent the blood tingling indignantly through her veins.

She reproached herself then for having accepted his

invitation. She really should have known better. He could keep his job, she decided, well-paid and inviting though it was, and in approximately two hours' time she would have the pleasure of telling him so.

If she had been able to communicate with Ivor over the noise of the motorbike, she would have told him about her date with the high-powered magazine publisher, but there was little point because she was going to turn the job down anyway. She couldn't work for a man like that.

Ivor dropped her outside her house and he told her he was busy that evening. 'Tomorrow any good?' he asked. 'No meetings to cover?'

She shook her head. 'Nothing to report.' They kissed quickly and he was on his way.

Her mother was in the kitchen. 'Don't cook anything for me, Mum,' Cleone called. 'I'm going out to a meal.'

'Are you, dear?' Her mother was surprised. 'Who with—Ivor?'

Cleone laughed. 'No. You know Ivor refuses to "waste" his money, as he puts it, on eating out. He prefers home cooking!'

Her mother laughed with her. 'He'll get that all right when he marries you, won't he?'

'If,' Cleone put in, and surprised herself by doing so.

Her mother came to the kitchen door. 'Oh? Having doubts?'

Cleone shook her head hurriedly and changed the subject. 'You won't believe who I'm dining with, Mum, and you won't believe me when I tell you why.'

'Well, go on, dear, don't keep me in suspense!'

'It's a man called Firse, Ellis Firse, owns a lot of magazines——'

Mrs. Aston could not have opened her eyes any wider if she had tried. 'My word, yes, I've heard of him.'

Cleone paused and eyed her mother doubtfully. How would she take the news? 'He's offered me a job—the editorship of a magazine.' Even as she said it, it seemed like an impossible dream.

Now her mother's mouth came open as well as her eyes, but Cleone rushed on, 'I'm turning it down, though. It doesn't appeal and it would be in London. I'd probably have to leave home . . .'

'Do you good, dear. It's time you did.' She put her hand on her daughter's arm. 'You can't turn down a good job like that, darling. Think about it. What a wonderful chance!'

'Dad won't like it. He never did want me to go into journalism, did he? Said it wasn't a safe job, or secure enough.'

'But, dear, even he wouldn't want you to throw away such an opportunity. I'm sure he'll think as I do about it.'

But her father did object, and strongly. 'I don't want a daughter of mine caught up in that rat race. You stay at home and realise when you're well off. I know you're an adult now, but you're still too young to come up against the types you'll find in that game. She's right to turn it down,' he told his wife. 'She's got more sense than I credited her with. She was a fool ever to go into journalism.' He turned to his daughter. 'Find a nice safe office job, where you can keep on working even after you're married.'

Cleone was sitting at the table drinking a cup of tea and watching her parents have their meal. She shuddered. 'A nice safe office job?' The very thought brought on a feeling of claustrophobia.

As she looked through the clothes in her wardrobe—she had made most of them herself—she thought of the contempt in Ellis Firse's eyes as he had enumerated the qualities he had considered essential for the job he was offering her. She would show Mr. Ellis Firse!

She drew out a white blouse which, because of the intricacy of its trimming, had taken her weeks to make. The neckline was high and throat-hugging and narrow strips of lace slanted diagonally at intervals across the front of the blouse from shoulder to waist. Between the lace insertions the material was caught into tiny tucks. The sleeves were full and narrowed into bands at the wrists, and the overall effect was young and appealing. She had made a skirt in black with touches of white here and there, and it contrasted dramatically with the blouse.

As she tugged the comb through her hair, she wished she could smooth away the cluster of curls which obstinately returned every time she washed them. With hair like that, she had given up long ago trying to look sophisticated.

At last she was ready and she looked critically at herself. 'If Mr. Firse doesn't like the way I look,' she thought disrespectfully, 'then he can just get lost!'

She swung out of the bedroom and down the stairs. Her mother caught her in the hall and praised her lavishly. It was just as well, Cleone thought, as she walked to the bus stop, because she certainly needed something to boost her confidence, although why she should feel so nervous when she was going to turn the job down, she could not imagine.

CHAPTER II

It was seven-thirty precisely when Cleone pushed through the hotel swing doors and looked round uncertainly for her host. Although she was accustomed to going about unescorted—her press ticket was a form of security and a passport to many unusual places—without its backing she felt shy and just a little daunted by the prospect of spending some hours in the company of a complete stranger, a man whose position was such that even her editor spoke about him in hushed tones.

She slipped out of her coat and draped it over her arm, but it was immediately lifted away by her host who appeared at her side.

He handed the coat to an attendant, then he smiled and said, 'Now what was the name—Cinderella?'

She made herself smile in return because it was polite to do so, but she knew he was referring to the incident of the sandal.

'Cleone Aston,' she said, her tone flat and cold.

'Ah, yes,' he replied. 'It's just as well because, alas, I'm no Prince Charming.'

She could not turn on that smile again, so she did not respond.

'Would you like a drink? No? You surprise me. Most of my lady guests can't wait until they have a glass in their hands.'

'I'm different,' she replied, trying to speak lightly.

'You are indeed,' he agreed, matching her tone.

He did not speak again until they faced each other across a table in the broad, high-ceilinged dining-room. He gave their order and as soon as the waiter left them she found herself saying,

'Mr. Firse, I'm sorry about what happened this afternoon.'

He laughed. 'You mean when you threw your shoe at me? I must admit that as an introduction to a woman, it was unique in my experience.'

She grew irritated. 'I didn't throw it at *you*, you know——'

He held up his hand. 'Don't spoil it. It's such a good story as it stands that it would be a pity to explain it away.' He looked at her, his eyes challenging. 'I won't sack you from my employ because of it.'

'Mr. Firse, I——' She stopped, her eyes down. She studied her reflection in the bowl of the spoon, noting abstractedly that it was staring back at her upside down. 'I've decided not to accept your offer.'

'I see.' He sounded cool, withdrawn.

She looked at him then, trying without success to read his expression. She wanted to stand up and say, 'There's no need to feed me now. I'll just say goodbye and go home.'

The waiter approached and Ellis Firse said, 'Good,

here's the food. Let's eat, then we can talk.'

The soup warmed her and brought colour to her cheeks and the tension began to filter out of her body.

He ran a practised eye over her clothes—she knew instinctively that he must have assessed many women in such a way—and said, 'You look very different from this afternoon. If you will forgive the question, where do you shop for your clothes?'

She answered with a flick of triumph, 'I make them myself.' But there was such an amateurish sound about the words that she immediately wished them unsaid. Now he would laugh, and that laugh would put her in her place—as an inferior, wage-earning, unsophisticated member of the female sex, beneath him financially, educationally and socially.

She rushed on, trying to deflect the blow his condescending smile would deal to her pride. 'Sometimes I buy a pattern and adapt it to my own ideas, or I design the things from scratch.' He was concentrating very hard on the candle flame which threw a flickering, unpredictable shadow over the table. He seemed quite uninterested in what she was saying, but her tongue fell over itself in an effort to explain, as though she had committed an anti-social act. Even as she spoke, she was annoyed with herself for making what closely resembled an apology.

'I like making things.' She realised she sounded defiant. 'I even make jam, cakes, bread sometimes...' She still could not be sure he was listening. 'I run a cookery column in the paper and do a weekly feature on dressmaking and fashion...' She tailed off.

She could see she was talking to herself. What had she expected—admiration? From a man with his power and his background to whom money was a means of obtaining everything he could ever want?

She went on defensively, 'I've had to do all these things because of financial necessity. One thing my parents and I have never suffered from is a surfeit of money.' It sounded almost like an accusation against him. 'Everything they've got they've had to struggle and save for.' She made no attempt now to keep the resentment from her voice. She looked at him, endeavouring to see how he was taking it, but his eyes were down and now it was his turn to study his inverted reflection in the bowl of his spoon.

'So,' she finished her monologue lamely, 'I make things. It's cheaper than buying them. And that way, you get the real thing, which I like.'

He said reflectively, proving he had been listening after all, 'The real fruit in the jam, real eggs in the cakes. No false colouring matter, no preservative. No pretence, no imitation, no artificiality.' He looked straight at her. 'As you say, the real thing.'

She flushed uncomfortably and was silent. They continued with their meal, not talking much, listening with a minimum of interest to the conversation around them. She wondered when he would start to put on the pressure to make her change her mind.

It was surprisingly pleasant sitting there with him. The strain she had anticipated was missing. Conversationally he did not force the pace. Now she felt she wanted to talk to him, to find a common interest and discover more about him.

'Have you any children, Mr. Firse?'

He laughed as if her question really amused him. 'I believe, Miss Aston, that even in these easy-going days, a necessary prerequisite to having a family is a wife. Like you, I'm not married.'

She was embarrassed and apologised, saying she didn't know, she had assumed he was married.

'Talking of marriage,' he said, 'was that your boy-friend calling for you this afternoon? You'll be marrying him soon, no doubt.' It was a statement, not a question. 'That's probably why you turned my offer down. I don't really blame you.'

She assured him quickly, 'No, that wasn't the reason. We

won't be marrying until we've saved enough to put down a deposit on a house of our own. We've got a long way to go.'

'And you're willing to wait?' He sounded surprised.

'Of course. Why not?'

He shook his head as though he could not believe his ears. They had their coffee in the lounge. They shared the couch and he motioned to her to pour out the coffee. As she handed him his cup he said, 'So you like your job on the local paper?'

'I love it. You meet people, go places. I like the freedom from four walls. When I go from one story to another, I walk rather than take a bus.' She laughed. 'You see, I like fresh air.'

He put down his cup and asked for more coffee. 'Do you—er—make a practice of walking barefoot?'

She looked at him quickly, then realised he was referring to what he had heard in the corridor that afternoon.

She coloured slightly. 'Well,' she said, defensive again, 'I like that too. I only do it over grass.' She smiled. 'It's such a pleasant feeling.'

'You wouldn't be able to walk barefoot over the pavements of London.'

It was a statement which required no answer. He said after a while, 'I believe we have a mutual acquaintance.'

She looked surprised, then said, 'Oh, you mean Mr. Riley.'

'No, I mean my grandmother.' At her puzzled glance he explained, 'Mrs. Firse, Bess Firse, the old lady you called to see today.'

Cleone's mouth came open with astonishment. 'Mrs. Firse—who crochets so beautifully?' Of course, why hadn't she recognised the name? 'My grandson,' she'd said, 'he comes to see me sometimes.' The other words came back, too—that he had half a dozen women friends and he 'loved them all'.

'How—how did you know I went there today?' She had

to give herself time to think, to sort out her thoughts.

'She said you were coming. You called there a couple of weeks ago, didn't you?' Cleone nodded, even more surprised. 'She told me that, too. You see, I'd told her I had a job to fill. She said she knew "a nice young lady on a local paper and why didn't I ask her?" ' He smiled. 'That "nice young lady" was you. That's why I came. I stay with her sometimes, and I've read some of your work in the paper. It's good. I didn't come after you today out of the blue. There was a method in my apparently haphazard behaviour.'

Cleone felt out of breath as though she had been running. 'Your father? She said he makes ladies' clothes.'

He laughed loudly at that. 'Yes, that would be how she sees it. He's a designer, a *couture* designer. You may have heard of him, despite your do-it-yourself activities. You might even have copied some of his designs.'

She shook her head. 'Firse? I've never heard of a designer called Firse.'

'No, not Firse. His real name is Francis Firse. But professionally he calls himself François.'

Cleone nearly dropped the cup she was holding. '*The* François?'

He nodded. '*The* François.'

Now the hand that held the cup felt weak. She lowered the cup to the saucer and returned them both to the tray.

'Your grandmother says she crochets the lace for her son—your father.'

'She does, but you must keep that strictly to yourself. We don't publicise the fact because the old lady would be besieged by the press and would-be customers. If the fact were known, she just could not cope. You do understand?'

'I understand.'

'Thanks,' he said briefly, and she knew he meant it.

They were silent again and she wondered when he would renew his offer. Perhaps he had no intention of doing so. Surprisingly, she started to panic.

'This job you offered me, Mr. Firse, what would it involve?'

He stretched out his legs and pushed his hands into his pockets. He was completely at ease. 'I see no point in discussing it. You've turned it down.'

It was like a slap in the face. She felt a thrust of anger and looked for her handbag. She lifted it on to her lap as if preparing to leave.

He watched her actions with interest. 'Anyway,' he said, and the word was lowered like bait into the river to catch her attention. It succeeded. 'I doubt if your personality would fit. I simply cannot see how we could turn a country kitten like you into a town cat. And I mean cat.' He smiled provocatively, dangling her on the end of the line. 'It would be cruelty to animals. You see, the type of women you would meet in such a job would tear a sweet, innocent young thing like you into tiny pieces. Those women have claws, sharp tongues and vicious natures.'

'But they can't all be like that. There must be some nice ones.'

He shook his head. 'I have yet to meet them. In any case, it's the nasty ones I'm concerned with. There are so many. I know what I'm talking about, Miss Aston. I've been in the game some time now.'

It seemed that he had written her off. Perversely she resented it.

'The magazine is small in size and limited in scope. We're concerned because its circulation is falling. It should be increasing. We want to halt the downward trend and we think the best way to do this is to recruit new blood.' For the first time that evening, he took out a cigarette. He offered her one.

'I don't smoke.'

'Wise girl. I don't usually, but now and then I feel the need. You don't object if I do?' She shook her head and he got the cigarette going with his lighter. He expelled the smoke and looked at her through it. He was obviously turning over in his mind his next words. He said, smiling, 'You don't drink much either, do you?'

'Not often.'

'Morals impeccable?' She flushed and he narrowed his eyes. 'Yes, I can see they are. No, you wouldn't fit in at all.'

She was angry again. 'I don't see what that's got to do with it. If the ability is there——'

He drew on his cigarette thoughtfully. 'Ah, but is it?' He released the smoke towards the ceiling and watched her speculatively.

She frowned. Was he playing with her, trying to provoke her?

'Of course it's there. I could easily tackle a job like that —if I wanted to.'

'You could?' The doubt was heavy in his voice, and he shook his head. 'You know, you weren't what I expected at all.'

'Well, what did you expect?' She was belligerent now.

'Something like the women I've just described.'

'Well, I'm sorry I disappointed you.' She looked at her watch. 'I mustn't detain you. Thank you for the meal, Mr. Firse.' She stood up and held out her hand. He ignored it and stood up, too.

'I'll take you home, Miss Aston, if you'll tell me how to get there.' He bent down and stubbed out his cigarette. She had a fleeting mental image of his large, luxurious car drawing up outside her parents' modest little house. 'No, thank you, Mr. Firse. I can find my own way back.'

He followed her into the entrance foyer. 'I insist, Miss Aston.' He waited while she found her coat and helped her on with it. 'My car is parked round the back.'

He put his hand under her elbow and propelled her outside. He held her so firmly she would have had to struggle to get away. He unlocked his car and let her in and she sank with a sigh into cushioned comfort.

His smile was gently mocking as he asked, 'My car meets

with your approval, despite its opulence?'

'It's wonderful,' she said with sincerity. 'If you have the money, of course you should buy the best.'

'I do agree.' He was smiling again. 'The very best. The real thing, in fact.'

He was laughing at her, gently, but she grew annoyed again. He held the ignition key in his hand and stared at it. 'Miss Aston, before I take you home, would you do something for me? Would you come with me to visit my grandmother? I'm not staying with her because I had no time to warn her of my arrival, but I promised to call in. I think she gets lonely sometimes, although she would never admit it. She says how much she loves seeing young people.'

The request surprised her, but her tone was even as she answered, 'Well, if it's not strictly a family affair, Mr. Firse, I should love to go with you. I think your grandmother's a wonderful person.'

He seemed pleased. 'Right. Then we'll go.' The car purred into life and moved towards the road.

'Your father,' he said, on the way, 'is he a journalist, too?'

She laughed. 'Good heavens, no. He's a local government employee. He's never forgiven me for going into journalism. At regular intervals he tries to persuade me to give it up and take a "nice safe office job" somewhere.'

'Did you tell him about our discussion this afternoon?'

'Yes,' she answered shortly.

'And what was his reaction?'

'He didn't approve.'

'Oh. Well, you've certainly got a lot against you, so it's as well you turned my offer down.'

'But I——' She frowned and found that her lip was trembling. Viciously she stilled it with her teeth and almost drew blood. Her eyes sought the soothing greenness of the countryside. She loved every inch of it. How could she ever think of leaving it?

Bess Firse's cottage had a low-hanging red-tiled roof

which dipped and curved with age. In the half-light of evening, its whitewashed walls glowed clean and bright. The iron door knocker was black and heavy to the fingers. The fingers that now raised it let it fall lightly back against the door, then they lifted the latch and pushed.

Ellis Firse motioned to Cleone to stay behind him. 'Grandmother?' he called, and went into the living-room.

'Ellis dear, come in, come in.' The thin voice wavered with pleasure.

He filled the doorway, keeping Cleone out of sight. 'I've brought you a visitor. A young lady, someone you know.'

'You have?' The voice was puzzled now, growing excited as she asked, 'Where is she?'

He walked in and Cleone followed. Mrs. Firse's mouth opened to speak, but she seemed too overwhelmed to form the words. Her pale cheeks grew flushed as she looked from one to the other. Her hand, shaking a little, came out.

'My dear child,' she looked at Cleone, 'come in. How sweet you look, how pretty.'

Cleone rested her hand in the outstretched one. 'Hallo, Mrs. Firse. I didn't expect to see you again today.'

'Nor I you, my dear. This is such a surprise.' Her eyes, sharp and questioning, turned towards her grandson. 'Ellis?' she asked.

'Miss Aston has been dining with me, Grandmother.' He sat on the arm of her chair and whispered in her ear, 'I've offered her that job.'

The bright eyes turned towards Cleone. 'And she's taking it? You're taking it, my dear?'

Cleone looked at Ellis. 'I—well, I——' How should she answer?

Ellis came to her rescue, his eyes warning her to give nothing away. 'She's thinking it over.'

'Oh, she'll take it. She'll accept, Ellis, I'm sure she will.'

He laughed. 'She will? You think I'm so irresistible, no woman could say no to me?'

'Now, Ellis, you're fooling. My dear child,' she spoke to

Cleone, 'sit here, on this.' Slowly her hand reached out and pulled the footstool towards her. Cleone sat at Mrs. Firse's feet and looked up into her face. She saw pleasure there and she could have sworn there were tears in her eyes. Was the old lady so lonely that she wept when people came?

She looked at Ellis, his arm resting lightly across his grandmother's shoulders, his affection for her giving warmth to his cool, controlled features and relaxing his austere, autocratic manner into an unaccustomed gentleness and approachability.

He caught her looking at him and smiled. It had a devastating effect on her and she experienced the most extraordinary sensation she had ever known. The room seemed to spin round and she had to hold her breath until it stopped.

Mrs. Firse was saying, 'I'm not going to call you Miss Aston, like my grandson. What is your name, my dear?'

'It's Cleone, Grandmother,' Ellis said. 'That's right, Miss Aston?'

She nodded, thinking how strange her name sounded on his lips.

'What a pretty name. Isn't it, Ellis?'

'It is indeed,' said Ellis, and smiled again. He whispered, 'Do you know what she did this afternoon, Grandmother, before we had been officially introduced? She threw her shoe at me!'

Two startled eyes, shadowed with age, opened wider. 'She didn't! You didn't, my dear!'

'Not really. I——'

'Oh, but she did. She can't deny it. I caught it right here.' He cupped his hands at his waist. 'You know, I nearly threw it back, but I just stopped myself.'

The old lady began to laugh; it was a quavering high-pitched laugh and she dabbed at her eyes as the tears began to form. 'Oh, my dear Cleone. Oh, Ellis,' she said, her voice steadier now. 'You cheer me up, Ellis. Every time he comes, Cleone, he makes me laugh.'

They talked then, about his mother and father and about his own affairs. When it was time to go, they went to the door and Mrs. Firse said to Cleone, 'I hope you'll come again, my dear. I get tired of my own company sometimes and it's good to see a young face now and then.'

Cleone promised that she would. Somehow she knew she would keep that promise. Mrs. Firse called her grandson back.

'Go out to my car, Miss Aston. I won't keep you more than a few minutes.'

So Cleone wandered out into the warm, dark evening and tried to throw off the sadness which had crept up on her. She wished she could prise it away, but no amount of reasoning could loosen its hold.

He was longer than she had expected. What were they talking about? Family business, she supposed, nothing whatever to do with her. She had an extraordinary feeling of regret at the thought. She wished he would hurry. She wanted to return to familiar surroundings, to the normal tranquillity of her emotions.

He came out at last, apologising, and took her home. Outside the house and over the quietly running engine, she said, 'Thank you for this evening, Mr. Firse. I'm—I'm sorry about refusing your offer——'

'That's all right, Miss Aston.' His tone was reasonable, unworried. 'I didn't make it for sentimental or philanthropic reasons. I'm a businessman pure and simple.'

That puts me right back in my place, she thought, as a passing acquaintance, a potential employee who said 'No, thanks' to the job. I'm no longer the privileged friend of the family. I've suited his purpose. I've cheered up his grandmother and that's that.

She ventured, 'Are you leaving in the morning?'

'Yes. First thing, probably. Why?'

'Oh,' she said hastily, 'it doesn't matter. Goodnight.'

He held out his hand. 'Goodbye, Miss Aston. I don't suppose we shall meet again.'

She put her hand into his for a few seconds, then got out of the car. Before she reached the front door, he had driven away.

Cleone had a restless night. By morning, she had made up her mind. She wanted that job. Not only was it a chance in a thousand, it was a challenge. She was sure she could do it. But it wasn't only that. Something else, some other factor had brought her to the decision. She couldn't pinpoint it, but it was there. And if her better judgment urged her to seize such a chance, who was she to argue with it?

She told her parents of her decision at breakfast. Her father said she was being a fool on two counts. One, in giving up her job on the local paper—'better the devil you know', he had said, and two, in taking on a job about which she knew next to nothing.

'Think of the types you'll be mixing with and working with. No morals, no scruples, and they'll make you the same.' He had made a noise of disgust and left for work.

Her mother approved. 'You've made the right decision, dear. I know you have. It's a wonderful opportunity. I suppose Ivor knows all about it?'

'Not yet. He may not like the idea.' She hoped he would not be awkward, though. When she told him the salary attached to the job, he would surely realise how much faster they would be able to save for their house.

She hurried to work and used the telephone in the reporters' room to phone Ellis Firse's hotel. They were sorry, they said, but he had checked out about ten minutes ago. Disappointed, she sat down and wondered how she could reach him. Mr. Riley might know his office number. She looked at the appointments diary and found she had an interview in half an hour. She would have to leave at once as it would take her all of that time to get there.

She was out for most of the morning. As soon as she arrived back at the newspaper office, she went to see Mr. Riley. Did he know Mr. Firse's business telephone number, she asked, because she had changed her mind about that job he had offered her. She was going to take it after all.

Mr. Riley looked at his watch. 'What a pity, you've missed him by barely half an hour,' he said. 'He called in to say goodbye before leaving for London.'

Cleone managed to hide her disappointment and asked, 'Did he—did he mention me, Mr. Riley?'

'No, my dear. Was there any reason for him to do so?'

She said she supposed there wasn't.

'You could probably find out his phone number from directory enquiries.'

After lunch she took his advice, and was given the information she required. As she dialled the complicated number and waited for her call to be answered, it occurred to her that she was trying to contact the top man in the firm—the managing director himself. She came up with a jolt against the barrier that formed suddenly in her mind and was in the act of putting down the phone when she was asked, 'Can I help you?'

She would like to speak to Mr. Firse, Cleone replied, Mr. Ellis Firse.

'I'll put you through to his secretary,' came the reply.

Seconds later she was asked again, 'Can I help you?'

Cleone repeated her question, 'Is it possible to speak to Mr. Firse?'

'No,' was the answer, 'I'm sorry, he's out. Would you try again later?'

Cleone fretted away an hour, then she dialled the number again and the whole performance was repeated. 'I'm sorry,' his secretary said, 'he didn't return when expected.'

Cleone said, as calmly as she could, that she would try again tomorrow. She nearly flung the receiver down in disgust. Thoroughly dispirited, she flopped into her chair and cupped her chin in her hands. She wished she could have been given yesterday back. How could she have allowed such an opportunity to slip through her fingers? She heard Ivor's motorbike revving outside, put on her coat and walked out to meet him. He left her at the gate, promising to call for her later.

She told her parents all about it. Her mother was disappointed, but her father cheered loudly. 'Give it up, girl,' he said. 'There's a reason why you couldn't get through to him, mark my words. There's a reason for everything.'

Cleone hoped he wouldn't start expounding his own particular philosophy of life at length, because she had heard it so many times before.

She went upstairs to get ready for Ivor, but felt little interest now in their outing. She wore a white sleeveless blouse with a scooped-out neckline and a navy skirt she had made herself.

Ivor was waiting for her in the dining-room. Hesitant and self-effacing as always, he was talking to her parents. Her mother's attitude towards him was protective, her father over-hearty to compensate for the young man's shyness. They both approved of him as a future son-in-law and thought their daughter's choice of him as a marriage partner had been surprisingly sound.

Cleone realised that in their life together she would always be the one to take the initiative. Sometimes the idea troubled her, but she supposed she would get used to it. She consoled herself with the thought that as Ivor grew older he was sure to become more mature and self-assertive.

He smiled his uncertain smile and brushed his thick fair hair in a nervous gesture. 'Ready?' he asked hopefully, as if anxious to escape from her parents' questions, which he clearly regarded as an inquisition.

He had left his motorbike at home, and they walked arm in arm to the bus stop. 'Where shall we go?' he asked, waiting as usual for Cleone to take the lead.

She suggested a film and Ivor agreed. Afterwards, when they were walking home she told him about Mr. Firse and his offer of a job. To her surprise, Ivor encouraged her to take it.

'It's so much more money than you're earning now—

more than I'm getting, in fact—that we'll be able to save up our deposit much faster.'

They parted, as they always did, with a gentle goodnight kiss.

Next morning Cleone phoned Ellis Firse again, but this time it seemed she was too early. He hadn't arrived yet, they said. She could have wept with annoyance.

His secretary asked, 'Shall I give him a message?'

'Yes, please. Would you tell him that Cleone Aston phoned?' She added with a confident smile, 'I think he'll know what it's about.'

Certainly, came the answer. How did she spell it? Cleone spelt out the letters of her name and, conscious of the mounting cost of her wasted phone calls, asked if he could ring her back when he came in.

'I'll certainly ask him, Miss Aston.'

Cleone had a morning free of appointments. She wrote up two or three stories and fretted away the rest of the time. She was so restless the others in the room grew impatient and told her to stop behaving like a tigress in the mating season.

Every time the phone rang, she tensed and pounced on the receiver before anyone else could do so. But Ellis Firse did not phone her.

It was nearly midday when, in desperation, she dialled his number for the last time. If he was not available now, she decided, she would give up.

'Yes,' his secretary answered, 'he's here. Would you like to speak to him?'

That, Cleone muttered to herself, is surely the question of the year. Her heart pounded like a roll of drums as she waited for him to speak.

'Ellis Firse here.'

She grew confused. 'This is—my name is—I mean I'm—this is Cleone Aston speaking.'

'Who?' barked the voice in her ear.

Oh, good heavens, had he forgotten her already?

'Miss Aston. Cleone Aston.' Her voice rose as she tried to get over to him who she was.

'Oh, Miss Aston. I see.' His tone was flat.

'Mr. Firse,' she fumbled for the right words, 'you remember that when you were here two days ago——' Is that all it was? she thought. No, two years, surely, '—you offered me a job?' Did she have to make it sound as if she were begging?

She waited for some response, but nothing happened.

She blundered on. If only he would help her out ... 'Well, I've changed my mind.'

'Oh.'

A single sound. As a reply it wasn't very helpful, but at least it proved he was still there. She knew it was a stupid question, but she asked, 'Is the post still unfilled?'

'In a sense, yes.'

What did he mean—'in a sense'?

'There's still time for you to apply for it, if you wish.'

Apply for it? But two days ago it had been hers for the asking!

'The interviews take place next week.'

Interviews? Now she was completely bewildered.

'Are you there, Miss Aston?' His voice was sharp.

'Yes, yes, please go on.' Her voice was hoarse.

'If you will send in your application straight away, addressed to me, giving the name of one person to whom we could write for a reference——'

But he'd had a reference—a verbal one—from Mr. Riley!

'—we'll let you know if you have been selected for an interview.'

Now she was shaking, not with nerves, but with anger.

'You understand, Miss Aston?'

Yes, Miss Aston understood. She said, her words clipped, 'I'll think it over and if I decide to apply, I'll write to you.'

'Yes, you do that, Miss Aston.' She could swear he was smiling. 'By the way, competition for the post will be formidable, so don't be surprised if you don't hear from us.'

She slammed the receiver down and curled her fingers as if she would like to choke him. So he was teaching her a lesson, was he? That evening, she filled both sides of a sheet of foolscap paper with her letter of application.

That should put Mr. Ellis Firse in his place, she thought, as she hammered down the flap of the envelope and went out to post it. Three days later she received a letter from the staff manager inviting her to attend for interview.

CHAPTER III

'You must have taken leave of your senses!'

Mr. Aston's parting shot to his daughter echoed through the hall as he left for work. He hoped she didn't get the job. Her mother went with her to the station, wished her luck and waved her off.

The confidence which had buoyed her up at the start of the journey ebbed slowly and painfully away as London grew nearer. Would she recognise Ellis Firse again? she wondered. She had almost forgotten what he looked like. He was tall, she remembered, much taller than she was. His eyes, which, with their brown colouring, should have been warm, were cool and detached, mirroring his whole personality.

His hair, she told herself, was thick and dark and tended to curl a little and if he had not kept it under control would have been unruly. Yes, she thought, she would know him when she saw him.

But when she did see him again, he looked remote and impersonal and was sitting at the far end of a long narrow table at the end of a long narrow room. It was a room that seemed to Cleone's nervous eyes to stretch without end into the far distance. A fine example of perspective if there ever was one, her fevered brain printed out to her, like a computer having its little joke.

There were faces on both sides of the table—five a side, six a side? She couldn't be sure. They were all masculine, weren't they? No, there was a woman amongst those men, hard-eyed, amply built, necklaced and ringed—the type Mr. Firse had so neatly described to her days ago—no, years ago—when she had dined with him.

'Sit down, Miss Aston,' said Ellis Firse.

There was not a flicker of recognition in his hard face. Where was the gentleness it had held that evening when he had looked down at his grandmother?

Miss Aston sat on the chair indicated. The questions began, slowly at first like gentle rain, increasing to the strength of hail pelting against a window. At first she answered with ease, becoming quite voluble in some of her replies. Those faces started to crease into the most grudging of smiles.

'Have you any domestic ties?' one of them asked. 'This is a demanding job and would require you to be easily available even in what is usually regarded as one's leisure time.'

'If you mean, "am I married?", then I'm not.'

'But, Miss Aston,' Ellis Firse's curt voice dug into her like a gun in her back, 'you're engaged, surely?'

'I'm—I'm not engaged, Mr. Firse. Not yet.'

His smile was cynical as though he was thinking, 'Here's another female who'll ditch a man if it suits her purpose.'

She blushed at the thought, but she had to acknowledge that this time he was right!

Then the bombardment began and the man in the forefront of the attack was Mr. Ellis Firse. One after the other his bombs burst dead on target. His questions blew her sky-high. How did she think, he wanted to know, with her quiet, country-style background, that she could possibly cope with the demands made upon her talents by London-based journalism? In other words, she thought, he's trying to say in polite terms that he doesn't think I'm good enough. And he was taking unfair advantage of his knowledge of her way of life.

She hissed in response like a cat about to sink its claws into an enemy. Of course she could adjust. It only required intelligence and determination. And she had plenty of that, hadn't she?

How, he asked, with her gentle upbringing and the almost paternal attitude of her present editor, did she think she was equipped to deal with the problems of the big outside world, the unpleasantness which would undoubtedly come her way, the criticisms, the dislike, the jealousy?

'How could you, with your lack of experience of the rough side of human nature, deal with the—I must say it—bitchiness of many of the people you would meet in the course of your work?'

She turned on him. She had stopped caring about the harm she might be doing to her cause. 'I too have claws, Mr. Firse. They may be hidden away, but I've got them and I keep them in trim and, when the occasion demands, use them most effectively. I'm no angel, even though I may look like one!'

There was a stunned silence, then a roar of laughter. Ellis Firse permitted himself to smile and told her she could go.

The last candidate went in and Cleone sat in the waiting room with the others. Her face was flushed, her heart was racing and the high neck of her blouse felt as if it was suffocating her. The others glanced up from their reading matter and looked her up and down. They were all, without exception, cool and calm. They were all of the type that Ellis Firse had described. She, with her fair skin only lightly made up, her simple self-made clothes, her uncertainty of manner, was the odd one out.

'I might as well go now,' she thought. She knew she had

not got the job. Ellis Firse, with his barbed questions and his drawing of blood, had seen to that. For some reason, and her eyes began to moisten at the thought, he had taken a dislike to her and didn't want her now.

The last girl came out. She was smiling and seemed pleased with herself. She was the one, Cleone decided, who would get it. She looked at her watch. She wouldn't give them much longer. There was a train in half an hour. She could just make it to the terminus if she hurried . . .

The door of the interviewing room opened. Ellis Firse stood there and stared straight at her. She stared back. 'Miss Aston!' He was calling her. Slowly she rose and walked towards him. He was only going to explain, to soften the blow. 'I'm sorry, but . . .'

She was standing in front of him. He bent his head slightly and whispered, 'Don't look at me as though you would like to throw your shoe at me again. I was only going to offer you the job!'

She swayed and he put his hand on her arm and pulled her into the room.

Later, in the train going home, she looked back on the events which followed, and they were a blur. Her hand had been shaken and shaken again. Ellis had asked her about accommodation and said they could probably arrange that for her if she wished. Someone else had said how nice it would be to have a fresh, young face to look at instead of . . . She hadn't heard the rest.

Ellis had said, 'I suppose they'll expect you to work out your month's notice? They wouldn't release you earlier?'

She didn't know, she'd said, but she would ask. He had seen her into a taxi and wished her a good journey home. She shut her eyes and rested her head against the back of the seat. The last thing she could remember was Ellis's face, watching as the taxi drove away.

Cleone called on Ellis's grandmother a few days before she

left to take up her new job. Mrs. Firse was delighted to see her.

'I hoped you would come and say goodbye, my dear.'

'Did you like the little piece I wrote about you in the paper, Mrs. Firse? I hope I got my facts right!'

'You certainly did. I was so pleased with it I sent a cutting to Ellis.'

'What did he think of it, Mrs. Firse?' She tried to keep the concern out of her voice.

'Oh, I haven't heard. He rarely writes. He leads such a busy life, as you will find out when you're working for him, won't you? I expect you'll see a lot of him.'

Cleone doubted that very much, but did not say so. 'Does he visit you often?' she asked, growing annoyed with herself for talking about him.

Mrs. Firse shook her head. 'Now and then.' She smiled and beckoned Cleone nearer. 'I'll tell you a secret. He usually comes when he's got a problem to solve. He tells me about it. You know, I really think it helps him just to talk. I rarely give an opinion, but he usually finds an answer.'

Her smile became a frown and the lines wrought by a long and full life were etched more deeply on her ageing skin. 'You see, he can't talk to his parents. His mother is pretty and charming, but hasn't a grain of sense in her head. His father—my son—well, I love him, my dear, but he is out of this world. His head is in the clouds—his work is his life. So Ellis comes to me.' She became reminiscent. 'He was such a dear boy in his childhood. He and I, even then, had a rapport, an understanding, which is only rarely found between two people at opposite ends of their life-spans. One day, I remember, he . . .'

As she talked about her grandson, Cleone became restless. She wished Mrs. Firse would stop. Hearing so many intimate details about Ellis Firse's childhood disturbed and worried her. It seemed to bring him there, make his presence almost real. She could visualise him sitting on the arm of his grandmother's chair smiling down at her, warm, human, loving . . .

She jerked herself out of her reverie and found herself laughing at something his grandmother had said. Before she left, Mrs. Firse held on to her hand. 'Come and see me again, Cleone, when you visit your parents. Have you got somewhere to live in town?'

'Yes, I'm having the flat vacated by Janice Smythe, the present editor of the magazine. Mr. Firse has arranged for the tenancy to pass to me.'

Mrs. Firse patted her hand. 'I hope you'll like the job.'

Cleone laughed. 'I expect I will. More to the point is, will Mr. Firse like me?'

'My dear child, there's no doubt about that, no doubt at all.'

Cleone thought, 'Wait until he's seen me in action. That's when his doubts will begin!'

On her last day at work, Mr. Riley presented her with an elaborate needlework basket. She said she would remember them all every time she used it.

One of the reporters commented, 'But you'll soon be earning so much money, you won't need to make your own clothes!'

Another said, 'Stay the nice girl you are, Cleone, although it won't be easy among the licentious lot you're going to work with.'

Mike, the tea-boy, had the last word. 'You'll have to learn the technique of keeping the wolves from the door, Cleone, or Ivor really will refuse to marry you!'

He ducked as she threatened to throw both her shoes at him.

The day Cleone moved into her flat, Janice Smythe moved out. They met at the door.

'You're welcome to the job,' Janice said. 'The only thing that's good about it is the salary. Which magazine do you come from?'

When Cleone told her that she had come from a local

newspaper, the other girl eyed her up and down. 'You're a country mouse and you think you can tackle this job! You won't last as long as I did. They give you a few weeks to settle in, then they start watching you. You don't know they're doing it. If you don't come up to scratch, you're out,' she snapped her fingers, 'just like that.'

'What do you mean—they "watch you"? Who does the watching?'

'Ellis, who else? He'll dine you and wine you and even take you out—it goes with the job—but all the time he's watching how you work.'

'But—but don't they leave you alone to get on with it?'

'You think they do, dear, but I swear he's got some built-in system of radar in there,' she tapped her head, 'and he does it so damned cleverly, you don't know he's doing it. I'll admit he's dishy to look at. He's not quite the country's most eligible bachelor, but not far off. And does he play on it! He collects girl-friends like a woman picks a bunch of flowers from her garden. But he's iron underneath that smooth exterior. You cross his path and you've had it. How did you get the job, anyway?'

Cleone told her.

'Now I get it,' Janice nodded as though everything was fitting into place, 'another of his "discoveries". I was one, dear. He met me at a party, offered me a job as a model in his father's *couture* house—I'd done some photographic modelling before. I took him up on his offer and worked for his father for a couple of years. Then his father changed his style and said my face didn't fit. So, on the assumption that I knew something about fashion, Ellis offered me this job. My face didn't fit here, either, so noticing the broad hints that were being dropped, I got myself another job. So enjoy it while you've got it. You won't have it long!'

Janice swept out, leaving behind a strong and slightly nauseating smell of perfume. Cleone sank into one of the deep cushioned armchairs. She closed her eyes as doubts and misgivings crowded in on her. What had she let herself in for? So she was one of his 'discoveries', was she? It seemed he made a habit of that sort of thing. It helped to put into perspective his speed in taking up his grandmother's suggestion of coming to see the 'nice young lady' who had interviewed her.

The thought depressed her to a surprising extent. It was not so much that her pride was hurt—which it was, 'serves me right', she thought ruefully, 'for being so vain'—but something else, something too elusive to pin down, some feeling she could not explain away.

During the evening she distributed her belongings about the flat, revelling in its comfort and spaciousness. It was better furnished and equipped than her parents' home and it was worth the rather high rent she would have to pay.

She phoned her parents and told them of her safe arrival. Then she rang Ivor and, as they talked, she visualised his face and gentle manner and was seized by a longing for him, for his solid familiarity and the security he represented.

It was strange next morning entering the editor's office—her office—and sitting at her own desk. She had arrived early to get the feel of the place before the other members of staff arrived. She tried to persuade herself that she was not nervous and that with practice and experience she would do the work as well as the next man.

She told herself that it would not take long to get used to the changed environment. She went to the window—the building was twelve storeys high—and looked down from the ninth floor on to the crawling traffic below. Her eyes lifted to gaze across London, over the church spires, famous landmarks and ancient buildings, dwarfed into insignificance by towering office blocks.

Here and there were oases of green, in the children's playgrounds and the leaves of the trees which had been allowed to remain standing by the land-hungry builders.

She turned away with a sigh. Green—it was a colour she was beginning to miss already. She sat down. There was an unnatural quiet everywhere. She smoothed the skirt of her new blue suit, chafing subconsciously against the fact that she had felt it necessary to boost her confidence by wearing an outfit she had bought rather than made herself.

Already she felt different and she was not sure that she liked it. With a nervous movement, she pulled towards her some back numbers of the magazine she had been employed to edit.

Salon, it was called. She didn't like the name any more than she liked the content and style. Since her appointment, she had studied the magazine in detail and every time she looked at it she felt that something was wrong.

There was a movement in the next room and Cleone tensed. The nervousness which had been dulled by the early morning silence of the building began to bite again.

There was a tap on the door. A face wearing a bright smile was pushed round it and a cheerful voice said, 'Good morning. May I come in? I'm your secretary. No, correction, I'm everybody's secretary.' The girl stood in the doorway. She looked at Cleone and Cleone looked at her. 'She's young,' they were both thinking, 'in fact she's my own age.'

Almost weak with relief, Cleone put out her hand and introduced herself.

'Hallo, Miss Aston,' the girl said. 'I'm Joanna Pleasance. Call me Joanna. Everyone else does.'

'I'm Cleone. Call me that. I don't like formality.'

'You know,' Joanna said, 'we've all been wondering who we'd get this time. We visualised—well, never mind. We're all young here and hoped it would be someone young like us. Take it from me, you'll be welcomed with open arms—where the men are concerned, literally!'

'Sit down,' Cleone invited, 'and tell me the set-up here.'

'There isn't a great deal to tell. There aren't many of us. Like me, we all do more than one job. Since there's no fashion editor, the editor usually does that job. Rick Walsh and Ben Harlow handle the art and advertising between them. Sarah Buckley's the sub-editor, but since there's precious little editorial space and she writes what there is herself, there isn't much for her to do! So she doubles up sometimes as fashion assistant. Then there's me. That's all. As you can see, small staff, small magazine.'

'And small circulation.'

Joanna made a face. 'You're right there. Every month when the magazine comes out, we wonder if it's going to be the last.'

Cleone was puzzled. 'But can't something be done about it? Can't the powers-that-be see there's something wrong?'

Joanna shrugged. 'You try telling them.' The phone rang. She stretched over the desk to answer it. 'Miss Aston's secretary.' She lifted her eyes to the ceiling, and handed the receiver to Cleone. 'Talk of the devil—the powers-that-be himself.' She went out.

'Ellis Firse here, Miss Aston.' So he had begun his watching brief already, had he? He hadn't even given her a chance to settle in before he started. 'How are you managing?'

'Very well, thank you,' she answered as if he had asked after her health. If he had enquired after her temper, the answer would have been different.

'Are you booked for lunch?'

'I don't think so.'

'Good. Then you can have it with me.'

'But, Mr. Firse, I really haven't the time——'

'Miss Aston, this is not a casual invitation. I'm not trying to make a pass at you.' She flushed with anger and clenched her teeth at the mouthpiece of the receiver. 'This is business.'

'I see,' she said icily, 'a royal command.'

'As you say, a royal command. I shall arrive at twelve-thirty sharp.' The receiver was slammed down at his end.

During the morning, Cleone met the other members of

the magazine staff. Rick was long, narrow and too good-looking to be true. Sarah was plump and cheerful and laughed at herself. Ben wore glasses and was, in his own words, an incurable pessimist.

She was alone when Ellis walked in. He stood still and looked at her.

'Dressed for the part, I see.' His smile irritated her. 'Both outwardly and inwardly.' He walked round the desk and looked down at her feet. 'M'm. Shoes on, too. That's a concession to her elevated position. She's coming on. The evolution is taking place. The country kitten is growing up.'

She fought with her temper and glared at him.

'I'm waiting,' he said, grinning.

'What for?'

'The shoe.'

'Mr. *Firse*!' She managed to make his name sound like an expletive. 'You gave me to understand that the object of this exercise was strictly business.'

'My word, she's even developed the executive manner, let alone the quelling executive eye!' He watched her temper flood her cheeks with colour. 'Forgive me, I was just reminiscing.' Even his apology mocked her. She would make him take her seriously.

'Personally, I would rather sit down here and now and talk . . .'

His manner became decisive. 'We will eat, then talk.'

The restaurant he chose was part of a famous department store whose name was internationally known. At first glance, there did not appear to be even one empty seat, let alone two. Ellis stood, tall and arrogant, with Cleone just behind him, in the doorway at the top of a short flight of steps. He waited until he was noticed and recognised. It took only a few minutes. A quiet word and a short walk later, after pushing between tables and retreating from stares, they were seated with due deference and flourish in a quiet corner at a table for two.

'Such,' Cleone reflected silently, 'is the power of wealth.'

He saw her secret smile. 'Don't say it,' he commented, 'I know what you're thinking.'

She shrugged. 'These surroundings are, I imagine, your natural habitat.'

'You don't like them?'

'It's not a matter of "liking" them. These people,' she looked round, 'they seem so unreal somehow, so artificial. Your sort, not mine.'

To her surprise, he did not rise to her challenge. He merely said, flatly, 'Don't tell me—not the real thing.'

Sorry now for her transgression into his private world and afraid that she had overstepped the bounds of propriety, she began to show appreciation of her surroundings. Who was she to criticise the places he patronised?

She looked at the menu—he had already ordered—and said, 'The food must be fabulous.'

He raised a sceptical eyebrow at her sudden enthusiasm, but said nothing. It was not until they were well into their meal that he started talking.

'Now,' he said, 'having partially satisfied our appetites and taken the edge off our tempers, I'll put you in the picture. You've no doubt had a chance to study the magazine by now and done some analysis on it?'

'Yes, I have,' she began, anxious to have her say, 'and I don't like——'

'Look, I said I would put *you* in the picture.' She said she was sorry and would not interrupt again until he had given her permission to do so. His eyebrow went up again at her sarcasm, but he let it pass.

'The set-up is this. I want you to take note of what I have to say, because it's very important. My father, as you know, has a *couture* business. His name, as you also know, is François, leader of fashion, dresser of beautiful and wealthy women. His designs are exclusive and very expensive. Consequently, his *clientèle* is small, so small in fact—and I'm going to be honest with you, because this is the point—that without outside financial backing he would not be able to continue. He would go bankrupt. The magazine you edit is run as a show-case for his work. That is its *raison d'être*.'

'You mean—it only exists to promote his interests, his business?'

'Yes.' He drank some wine and put down his glass with a decisive thump. 'Because of its aims, its circulation is restricted. Its purpose is to attract those women—women with rich husbands, and there are still many—who live in the provinces and are too shy,' he saw her unbelieving frown, 'yes, I mean shy, to come to *couture* houses such as my father's. It acts, if you like, as a sort of carrot, an inducement to them to patronise him.'

His expression changed. He dropped his autocratic air, looked down at the empty glass he was holding. 'I feel you should know,' he sounded uncharacteristically hesitant, 'that financially, my father's business is in a bad way.'

She had the feeling that he was not talking to her now as an employee but as man to woman.

With his guard lowered, his expression looked strangely vulnerable, and compassion touched her as light as a snowflake. The antagonism which she felt whenever she was near him melted away and she wanted to reach out and cover his hand with hers. He looked up and caught her eyes on him. That feeling, it was there again. Her senses reeled as they had done that day he had smiled at her in his grandmother's cottage. The room spun round and she went with it.

She fought for composure and after a short interval heard him say, '*Couture* generally is feeling the effects of the changing times, so his is not an unusual experience.'

'Mr. Firse,' she said, and his eyes flickered up to hers and down again, 'may I——' She stopped, selecting her words carefully because she knew it was not really her business, but she had to know. 'May I ask if you're the owner of the firm?'

He didn't seem to mind her question. 'No. My father

owns both the *couture* business and the publishing side. You see, my uncle—his brother—died, leaving the publishing firm to my father.' He smiled grimly. 'My father's a hopeless administrator, so I moved in and took over. I manage it for him. He struggles along with his *couture*. A percentage of the profits produced by the publishing business helps to cover my father financially.'

'Has your father any sidelines, like other *couturiers*? Cosmetics, for instance, perfume, jewellery...?'

'No. Where his business is concerned, my father's a purist. He refuses to accept that it cannot stand on its own feet without "crutches", as he puts it, such as you've mentioned. He dismisses them as props, gimmicks, to disguise a designer's incompetence.'

'That simply isn't true,' she protested. 'Think of the famous designers who have given their names to other things——'

'His mind is closed on the subject.'

'But surely you, as a businessman, can talk him round——'

'I'll introduce you to my father, Miss Aston. Then you'll see that not only is it impossible to "talk him round", as you suggest, it's almost impossible to communicate with him. It's as though he lives on a different plane from the rest of us, in a world of his own.'

'And another thing,' her cheeks were growing flushed with enthusiasm for her subject and she did not notice his eyes watching her, 'nearly all the well-known designers nowadays run boutiques, have ready-to-wear ranges. They adapt their own original designs or get one of their design assistants to do it for them.'

'You're telling me something I already know, Miss Aston.' His voice had an edge to it now, but she refused to acknowledge it.

Unconsciously she started to plead, 'Mr. Firse, the magazine—as it stands—won't last more than a few months. It's got to be altered to save its life. I've got so many ideas,' she saw with dismay that his eyes were assuming their customary hardness, 'and if I could be allowed to make changes, gradually of course . . .' Her voice tailed off, uncertain, unsuccessful, as his expression brought to an abrupt halt her evangelical attempt to convert him to her point of view.

'It seems as though I shall have to repeat myself *ad nauseam*, until the message is received,' he said coldly.

They had returned to the employer–employee level. She was back in her place and could not contradict.

'The magazine will remain in its present form. Neither its format nor its contents will be changed.'

Now he was every inch the autocratic head of the firm. He was dictating policy and she had to accept or resign. Reluctantly and, she promised herself, for the time being only, she accepted.

They finished their meal in silence. The coffee did nothing to thaw the cold truce between them. He looked at his watch.

'Have you any appointments this afternoon? No? Good. I'll take you to my father's *couture* house. Sooner or later you will have to meet him and as you are, in a sense, a *protégée* of mine, I'd better take you myself. Are you ready?' He rose and helped her with her jacket and settled the bill.

The house was painted white. 'White,' she thought, 'like his grandmother's cottage.' But it resembled the simplicity of the old lady's home in no other way. It was large, Georgian and just a little intimidating when she thought about the famous man who lived in it.

Above her head an ornate doorway led on to a balcony which spanned the first-floor windows. Two white stone columns rose impressively on each side of the entrance doors. The small front gardens were a mass of orange roses and it was a fitting residence, Cleone decided, for such a man as Ellis's father to make his home. A place for a man to dream in and to hide in away from the everyday world.

The entrance hall was spacious and formal, with its red floral patterned carpet, the highly polished wooden tables and antique chairs. The lighting was soft and subdued. Paintings hung on the walls. The staircase rose from a central point and divided into two separate approaches to the landing. This, Cleone imagined, was surely where François staged his fashion shows.

'Suitably impressed, Miss Aston?' Ellis asked, smiling sarcastically. He pointed to the paintings. 'The real thing.' He indicated the flowers in giant vases and the shining brass containers placed at intervals on the recessed window-sills. 'The real thing,' he repeated, watching her irritation grow. He nodded towards the carpet. 'You could even go barefoot, if you wanted to.'

She didn't answer, she just looked at him, but he was not in the least abashed. He smiled tauntingly and told her to follow. 'I seem to have done nothing else since I met the man,' she reflected irritably. 'He leads, I follow. It's a wonder he doesn't put a collar round my neck and pull me behind him on a leash.'

They went up the staircase and rebelliously, Cleone trod behind him. She stifled an urge to go up the other side if only to prove to him and herself that she still had a will of her own and was not simply his shadow.

'Wait there,' he said sharply, pointing to a high-backed wooden seat. There was an edginess about him that touched a responsive chord in her and for once she did not resent his curtness. She became tense in sympathy with him and when he beckoned her into the room she gave him a tight smile. He did not smile back.

'My mother,' he said, his face wooden. 'Mother, Miss Aston.'

She was small built and slim, her clothes were François-designed and *couture*-cut to the last inch of fabric. Her hair was white and set to perfection. Her eyes held a hopeless, waiting look and when she spoke it was with the high whining voice of a child who had been ignored for years and had taken to complaining to attract attention. To have said that they shook hands would have been to invest the action with a vigour which was just not there. It was rather a touching of fingers.

Cleone smiled and thought, 'Well, someone's got to smile sooner or later.' There seemed to be no one else who was prepared to bring some warmth into that emotionally frozen climate.

Emilie Firse did not speak to Cleone. She addressed her son instead. 'Your father is coming in a few minutes. At least, that is what he said, but you know he never comes when he says he will.'

'Sit down, Miss Aston,' Ellis said with a sigh. 'It seems we may have a long wait.' He strolled to the window, taking out a cigarette on the way. He still appeared to be on edge. If he could not relax in his parents' home, how, Cleone wondered, could she, a complete stranger?

The door opened and François walked in. Ellis turned, introduced them and watched as their hands met. François put no more friendliness into the action than his wife had done.

His hair was grey and he wore it rather long. He was of medium height—how did their son grow so tall? Cleone thought—and his face, though handsome for a man of his age, was cold and devoid of life. 'Is this what their son will be like when he is middle-aged? He's on the way to it now.' She checked her thoughts and produced the smile again.

It was ignored and died on her lips. She was being inspected by those cold blue eyes with suspicion and distaste. He was looking at her as a child regards a stranger standing on the doorstep and who is threatening to invade his home. His eyes were blinking a little as he looked her over like someone who had just emerged from the darkness and was troubled by a bright light.

He sat down and, like his wife, waited. Cleone grew desperate. Someone had to break that strangling silence. What about the weather? Their health? Her work?

'This house,' she said, with concentrated enthusiasm, 'it's wonderful. It's beautiful.'

Mrs. Firse moved impatiently, providing at last a positive response. 'You like it? It's too big,' she whined. 'I should like to move. I should like to separate the business side of my husband's work from our private lives . . .'

'This house,' said François, 'is perfect. For the purposes for which we require it, it could not be bettered.'

There ended the conversation. Cleone felt herself growing hysterical and looked imploringly at Ellis. Why didn't he help? But he was lounging against the windowsill, detached and indifferent. Only the way he drew on his cigarette, inhaling deeply and slowly releasing the smoke, only the guarded watchfulness of his eyes betrayed his tension. No link, no common bond seemed to draw them together, not even real affection. There seemed on his part to be only a strong sense of filial duty, coupled perhaps with a kind of protectiveness towards his father.

'He can't talk to his parents,' his grandmother had said, 'so he talks to me.'

'My father,' he had told her over lunch, 'lives in a world of his own. It's impossible to communicate with him.' Now she understood what he meant. As she tried without success to make contact with the great designer, she acknowledged that such a man would surely never change his ways. He was like a captain who chose to go down with his ship rather than make an effort to save himself.

Still they were watching and waiting. She tried to speak again, but could not form a single coherent sentence in her mind. She turned appealing eyes to Ellis. He was looking at her, his eyes like flint. He drew once more on his cigarette and tossed it into the empty grate.

He threw into the silence, 'She knows Grandmother.'

There was a flicker of response from François. 'Is she well?'

Like a child who had been offered a sweet, she grabbed at the subject and, with an eager tongue, made the most of it.

'She's fine,' she enthused, 'she's a wonderful person. I called to see her and she told me her story. The lace she makes——'

François asked sharply, 'You know about the lace?'

'She does,' Ellis answered for her.

'Then please, Miss—er—Miss Aston, keep it to yourself. Not a word to anyone.'

She assured him that she had already given her promise to his son about that.

'And how did you meet my mother?'

'Before I came to work for'—she looked at Ellis—'for your son, I was a reporter on the local newspaper. I——'

'You're a *reporter*?' It was almost a shriek from Emilie Firse. 'I thought you had come to do some modelling!'

If François' eyes could have grown colder, they would have done. 'We do not like reporters in this House.' And he meant the House of François, not the home he lived in. The look which he turned on his son reprimanded him for bringing such a creature into the place.

'Father,' said Ellis, his tone patient and slow, 'Miss Aston is the new editor of *Salon*.'

The information seemed to make no difference to the designer's ill-humour. 'Even the editor of *Salon* is welcome in my House only when the need arises, and that is at the showing of my collection. I simply do not trust any representative of the press, whoever he or she may be.'

'But, Mr Firse, you should like them,' Cleone cried, her tongue loosened as she tried to batter her way into his private world. 'In between collections they could make your business for you, if you would let them. Their backing, the publicity they could give you, would take away your financial worries and give you an assured future.'

'Miss Aston, I do not need an inexperienced young girl like you to tell me how to run my business. I get all the publicity I need from *Salon.*'

She ignored his acid tones and the rebuke in his words. In her earnestness, she was aware only that she was at last communicating with him, even though it was like shouting across a wide, dangerous river.

She shook her head. 'We don't give you publicity, Mr. Firse, not the sort I mean. How can we, when our freedom to print what we want is so rigidly controlled?'

The designer seemed too astounded by her impudence to interrupt. His son stood by, his lips tight, his eyes betraying the struggle within him.

She went on, her fervour making her oblivious of the undercurrents, 'We're fed editorially by you. My colleagues tell me that we're restricted in what we can say, and that we're only allowed to use photographs of your designs which you have selected. Apparently, we have no choice in the matter. And they tell me we're only allowed to print them anyway because as designs they're out of date and finished by the time we get them. All *Salon* is really is just a glorified catalogue.'

François stood. He was shaking with anger, his face wiped clean of colour.

Ellis was at her side in a few strides and bruising fingers closed over her arm. 'Miss Aston!' It was a warning, an angry warning.

'I'm sorry, Mr. Firse.' She was pale now, and frightened, too.

The door burst open. A distraught woman begged, 'Monsieur François, come quickly. Annabelle is crying and I cannot get her to stop.'

Ellis asked sharply, 'What's the matter with her?'

'She says I work her too hard, that I expect too much, and now . . .' She moved her hands in despair.

'I'll pacify her,' Ellis said. 'I'll come and calm her down.' And he was gone.

Still pale, and walking round her as though she had a contagious illness, François followed his son. Cleone turned to Mrs. Firse to renew her apologies, but Emilie took up her book and left the room.

Cleone was alone. Weak now with reaction, she sank on to a chair and held her head. 'If I don't get out of this house soon,' she thought, 'I'll go crazy!'

'Mademoiselle Aston?' The distraught *vendeuse* with the French accent was standing in the doorway. 'Mr. Firse, he says, will you come?'

She followed the short, plump figure along the corridor, down some steps and into another part of the house. As the door to the workrooms opened, the sound of weeping came through.

A slim, beautiful, partly dressed young woman was crying with determined abandon in Ellis's arms.

CHAPTER IV

CLEONE could only stand and watch as Ellis stroked the soft fair hair and tightened his hold as the crying started again, after the minor interruption of Cleone's entry.

One of his women, she supposed, and wondered why she felt so miserable. Where were the other five? She looked round, but could see no more models. 'Perhaps they're hiding amongst the racks of clothes and waiting their turn to be loved.' The stupid thought nearly made her laugh, then she wanted to cry. 'I'm getting hysterical,' she decided, and turned with relief when someone said,

'Hallo. Have you come to model? You're a bit small for that, aren't you?'

She walked across to the young man who had spoken, and was conscious of Ellis's watching eyes.

'No,' she laughed, 'I'm a journalist.'

He lifted his head—a well-shaped head with delicately moulded features and a rather feminine mouth—and put on an expression of amused disgust. 'One of those. We don't like them here.'

'So I gathered from—from...'

The girl had stopped crying and was dabbing carefully at her eyes with the handkerchief Ellis had lent her.

The young man helped her out. 'From the powers that be? Yes, you won't be popular in that quarter. My name's Antoine, by the way. Anthony really, but we all have to be French in this House.' He lowered his voice. 'Emily's become Emilie, Frank's François, Anne there,' he indicated the model, 'is now Annabelle, and so on. If you hang around long enough—which being a journalist you won't be allowed to do—heaven knows what they'd do with your name. What is it, by the way?' She told him. 'Cleone?' Ellis looked up sharply. 'I like that, very much.'

'Miss Aston,' came Ellis's cold tones, 'I suggest that you allow Antoine to get on with his work.'

'Oh, it's all right, Mr. Firse,' Antoine assured him, 'I'm not doing anything which needs a lot of thought.' He smiled at her and she smiled back. 'My goodness,' he commented, 'the atmosphere's warmed up a bit since you came in. Like the promise of spring after a long, long winter.'

She laughed and Ellis's frown grew deeper. 'Are you a designer?' she asked.

'One of these days I hope to be just that.'

'You're an apprentice, then?'

'In a way. Academically, I'm qualified. I graduated from college, but here I've had to start from scratch, running round after the great man himself and feeling honoured to be allowed to pick up his pins, if you know what I mean.'

'What are you doing now?'

'Taking a *toile* to pieces. You see, first we make sketches and the customer chooses her design from those. Then we make the *toile* out of calico. She tries on the *toile* for a fitting, then we take it to pieces and use it as a pattern.'

'Miss Aston,' she heard the impatience in Ellis's voice and turned. 'We have to go.'

'Ellis,' Annabelle's arms went round his neck, 'don't go

yet, please.'

He leaned forward and touched her forehead with his lips. Gently he loosened her hold. 'I have to, sweetie. I must take Miss Aston back. She has work to do.'

'Then come back later, Ellis.' The pleading note was there again. Her arms threatened to creep back round his neck and he moved out of range.

'Elusive,' thought Cleone sourly, 'must be his second name. I suppose, if he has six women on his list simultaneously, he can't make himself too readily available to any one of them.'

'Ready, Miss Aston?'

Annabelle turned at the sound of Cleone's name and the large eyes that inspected her were tinged with disdain. But Cleone saw only the faultless figure of the girl who was looking at her, and the charm of her perfect features.

For no reason at all, Cleone felt a thrust of anger. Deliberately turning her back and determined to show him she was not a domesticated pet he could call to heel at will, she walked across to some shelves which were stacked high with cloth.

'What fabulous material!' She handled a corner with expert, appreciative fingers. 'But why is it tucked away in a corner?'

'It's awaiting the approval—or disapproval—of the lord and master,' said Antoine, blandly ignoring the lord and master's son, whose mouth was beginning to tighten ominously. 'Fabric houses send it in, hoping and praying it will be chosen for some of François' designs. If it is, the manufacturers are made, because the fabric will be bought all over the world—a sort of seal of approval by a great designer. Sometimes it takes him months to get round to deciding whether to accept or reject it. In the meantime, they dare not send it anywhere else in case he says "yes".'

She ran the palm of her hand lovingly over one of the rolls of cloth.

'That fabric is strictly private!' She swung round and

saw the pale, angry face of François himself. 'It is not on public view—especially to the press.'

'*Miss Aston!*' Ellis shouted. This time she went scurrying to heel like a puppy being threatened by a St. Bernard.

'Goodbye, Cleone,' Antoine called, but Ellis made sure that she was not given the chance to answer.

In the car, she expected retribution, but it didn't come. Instead he said, surprisingly, 'I'm sorry about that episode.'

She looked startled. 'I thought I should be the one to apologise.'

'What for?'

'My outburst. I just couldn't help it, Mr. Firse.'

He shrugged. 'It was not unexpected. Perhaps it needed saying.'

'Is that why you took me?'

'Not exactly.' He concentrated on the traffic ahead. 'What did you think of my parents?'

She was surprised that he wanted her opinion, but what could she say?

'Be honest. You usually are.'

Taken aback by his bluntness, she said, 'They're—rather difficult.'

He laughed. 'A superb understatement!' He became serious. 'For my part, I've given up trying to find a way through to them, especially my father.'

Thinking the subject should be changed, she said casually, 'Annabelle is beautiful.'

'She is. I found her in a rather low-class retailers, acting as a salesgirl-cum-model. I realised her potential and offered her a job with my father.'

'Another of your protégées? Do you go round looking for them?'

He laughed and answered cryptically, 'I certainly don't go around with my eyes shut.'

'First you find them, then you elevate them, then you make them your girl-friends.'

He laughed again. He seemed to have quite thrown off

his edginess. 'Now that's a leading question.' He threw her a provocative glance. 'After all, I found you.'

'I was just wondering what your strategy was, so that I know what's coming to me.'

'Ah, but,' he stopped at a pedestrian crossing, 'I never have a fixed strategy where women are concerned.' He flicked an irritating smile at her rigid profile and drove on. 'Whenever I meet a new female who takes my fancy, I usually play it by ear.'

'In other words,' she snapped, 'you feel your way.'

'You couldn't have put it more aptly,' he answered, grinning.

She clenched her fists. He saw the action and laughed.

They had arrived at the office and his car slid to a standstill in a parking bay labelled dauntingly, 'Managing Director'. It reminded Cleone politely but pointedly of her position as a mere employee.

'Thank you for the lunch, Mr. Firse.'

He bowed his head with mock graciousness. 'Thank you for your charming company, Miss Aston.'

'We—we didn't come to any conclusions, did we?' He raised his eyebrows. 'About the magazine.'

'As far as I'm concerned, the matter is closed.'

'But, Mr. Firse . . .'

He looked at his watch. 'I have another appointment.'

She got out of the car and went in.

That evening, she phoned Ivor. They talked for a while and she told him she was longing to see him again. She promised to try and get home for a weekend before long.

'I'll give you my phone number, then you can ring me some time.'

But he told her he wouldn't do that since he never knew when she would be in. 'You phone me,' he said.

She rang off with a sigh, wishing once again that he would take the initiative now and then.

Next day she called an editorial conference. Rick wandered in, sat in a chair and lifted his feet on to the desk, asking beforehand, with mock formality, for Cleone's permission to do so.

Sarah sank into the armchair, saying it was so low and she was so fat she would never get up again. Ben Harlow turned the waste paper bin upside down and sat on it. Joanna trundled her own chair in and sat, notebook in hand, to take the 'minutes'. Rick said that since they were all so talkative, it was more likely that she would be taking the 'hours'.

Cleone acted as chairman and she let them all have their say. One by one they tore the magazine to shreds, criticising its style (which they said had been forced on them by the management), its content, its presentation and its pandering to one type and class of woman. Under it all, Cleone could detect anxiety—for the future of the magazine, and for their jobs.

Even the advertisements, they said, were vetted by Ellis Firse on behalf of his father. Couldn't she do anything, they asked with desperation, couldn't she, as a newcomer, try to talk him round to their point of view and make him see reason?

'I tried,' she told them, 'only yesterday, but he wouldn't listen. But I'm willing to have another go.' Impulsively she dialled his extension on the internal telephone. The offices of all the top people in the firm were on the ground floor.

'No,' his secretary said, as brightly as ever, 'I'm sorry, but he's out.'

Was the man never in? She slammed down the phone and they sat gloomily staring at each other, awaiting inspiration. Nothing happened and they all began to laugh.

'I'll make some tea,' Joanna said. 'That might cheer us up.'

As they drank it, sharing Sarah's packet of biscuits, Cleone told them how unpleasant François had been to her when he had discovered who she was. She couldn't understand his attitude, she said. 'After all, I'm supposed to be on his side, representing his interests.'

'He doesn't trust any journalist, no matter who it is,' Sarah said. 'He's scared stiff of piracy—you know, of his ideas being stolen, but he's no different from other designers. Usually the only time they welcome the press is at the showing of their collections.'

'Well,' said Cleone, 'where the magazine's concerned, I refuse to give up hope. I'll just have to tackle Mr. Firse again and keep on at him so much that he'll get fed up and give in——'

'And give the editor notice to quit, you mean,' Rick said, and they all laughed.

The door opened and Ellis Firse asked scathingly, 'Don't you ever do any work on this floor?'

The others melted away and Cleone was left alone to take the rap.

'I understand you rang me,' he snapped.

'Yes, Mr. Firse.' She hesitated, cursing the bad start. Now he was in quite the wrong mood to see reason. 'I wondered if I could talk to you.'

'What about?'

'About the—the——' Not daring to say the word, she held out a copy of *Salon*. Something in her eyes must have found a small pocket of warmth inside him, because he looked at his watch and said, 'Come down to my office in five minutes.'

Five minutes later, she was sitting on the other side of his desk eyeing him apprehensively. His expression reminded her of the day she had been interviewed for the job. He had given her hell then. Was he all set to repeat the performance now?

Seeing her embarrassment, he gave her a lead. 'What's this, a deputation of one? You've been here two days and already you're leading a rebellion.'

At least his mood seemed amenable. He had not shut his ears to her yet. He went on in the same half-joking manner, 'If it's not a rude question, what was that tea party on the ninth floor in aid of?'

She answered primly, 'It was an editorial conference.'

He shouted with laughter. 'Now tell me another!'

'Yes, I will, Mr. Firse. They were a group of thoroughly dissatisfied people.'

'Were they indeed! What about? Aren't they being paid enough?' His mood had changed and he was being sarcastic.

'Money doesn't come into it.'

'That's a relief!'

'Not in the sense you mean. Perhaps it does in other ways, though.'

'I'm all ears.'

That was her cue. She took a breath and made her entrance. It had to be a good performance.

'We should like to change the style of the magazine. We should like to make it bigger in size.' She saw the sceptical lift of the eyebrow and knew she had not made a very good start. 'It's too limited in scope and is aimed at a too-specialised market. We want more editorial matter—at the moment, it's cut to a minimum.' She consulted her notes. 'The advertising matter is grouped into a solid mass. We think it's indigestible to the mind and repellent to the eye.'

He settled back in his chair with a slightly bored expression as if he could only just bear to hear her out. She decided on attack and brought up reinforcements.

'We consider that it caters,' she used the editorial 'we' deliberately, 'for the sort of woman who exists only in your father's ageing imagination.' He stiffened perceptibly and she knew she was at last getting his full attention. 'The sort of woman who is well-bred—there are precious few of those women around these days, even in your income bracket,' now she was goading him, but she didn't care, 'running over with excess cash—they would need to be to pay your father's prices—so much so that they don't know what else to do with it, so they spend it on clothes. They have nothing else to do, so they pass their time having fittings at their *couturiers* and boasting about it afterwards.' She shook her head. 'It just doesn't happen that way any more.'

He tried to interrupt, but she pressed on, 'All the signs are pointing to the fact that *couture* is slowly but surely on its way out. The top designers these days have their ready-to-wear ranges, clothes which they have designed especially for the retail markets. They've been forced to do this partly for financial reasons and partly because of changing tastes and needs, so your father will have to give in in the end. Whether he likes it or not, one day he may even have to branch out into perfumery and cosmetics as many of the other *couturiers* have done.'

She paused for the breath she urgently needed for the final run-up to the tape. 'Your father lives and works in a vacuum, which no designer should ever do. Why, even your grandmother has a greater appreciation of the changing ways of the world than he has.'

She watched his mouth thin into a tight line. He was feeling the blade of a letter opener as if testing it for sharpness. Speculatively he eyed her throat.

Disregarding the warning signs, she raced to the end. 'Nowadays clothes are fashioned for the way people live. They aren't formal or pretentious any more. We want our magazine to mirror the times, as all fashion does. We want ordinary people to read it. We would like to introduce a beauty section and an accessories page. There's no fiction, nothing of general interest, precious little editorial matter. How it achieved any circulation at all beats me.'

She sat back, ready for the consequences. He threw down the letter opener and straightened up. 'I'm sorry, Miss Aston, it's just not on. The management would not—in the circumstances, the special circumstances—agree to such a drastic alteration in the magazine.'

She rallied. 'But, Mr. Firse, those people up there on the ninth floor, they've got enthusiasm, team spirit, they *want* the magazine to succeed. Doesn't that count for anything? It's not just that they're worried about their jobs—which they are—but it would give them a sense of achievement, of fulfilment, if the sales of *Salon* were to go up, even if only by a few dozen copies.'

He appeared completely unmoved.

'All we're asking for, Mr. Firse, is more pages, more colour and more scope.'

'Not much, is it, Miss Aston? You've forgotten the two vital words—more money.'

'And it's not available?'

He sidestepped in his answer. 'It's not simply a question of money. It's policy. The management would never agree.'

'You mean,' she cried, tears moistening her eyes as she sensed defeat, 'your father would never agree, *you* would never agree.' She disregarded the hardening of his eyes. '*You*, protecting your father's interests. Or that's what you think you're doing. But you're quite mistaken. By not challenging him, as I did, by giving in to his obstinacy, by standing back and shrugging your shoulders over him as I've seen you do, and saying you've given up trying to "reach" him, you're actually doing him harm.'

She could not make herself look at him. If she saw his eyes she knew they would freeze her into silence. 'If he were anyone but your father, if you were dealing with him as a cold-blooded businessman deals with a comparative stranger, you wouldn't tolerate his old-fashioned ideas for one minute. You'd be quite brutal and threaten to withdraw all financial backing unless he agreed to change his ways.'

Now he started to talk and she had to listen. 'I'm touched indeed, Miss Aston, that after so short a time with the company—forty-eight hours, is it not?—you have our interests so much at heart. But I would remind you that you have not been appointed to the staff to act as a financial adviser. You're an employee, just one amongst hundreds, and as such,' he took a breath and said through his teeth, 'you—are—*expendable*!'

But she still refused to give in. 'You can try to muzzle

me by threatening me if you like, Mr. Firse,' she cried, 'but it's the truth, and like everyone else, you don't like the truth!'

She fled from the room.

Another issue of *Salon* was almost ready for the printers. As it was a monthly magazine, it had been prepared in advance and most of the work on it had been completed before Cleone had taken up her job. When she saw it taking shape, she despaired.

'The same old thing served up at regular intervals,' Sarah groaned as they flicked over the rough pages.

Cleone made a secret vow that she would alter that magazine somehow, even if it cost her her job.

She spent the next few days attending fashion shows in the large stores, looking round their dress departments and seeking out the young people's boutiques which had appeared in different parts of London.

As editor of *Salon*, she received invitations to private shows. Some of these she attended with Sarah, and some alone. One invitation requested her presence at a shoe collection in a well-known hotel. The designer was in attendance with his assistants and he was overflowing with good humour and willingness to please. Buyers, representing wholesalers and stores, were eager to see the latest styles and were pushing against each other to get a better view of the shoes on display.

Cleone was penned in like a sheep being taken to market. She tried to acclimatise herself to the chaos and felt herself growing as excited as everyone else. But after half an hour of it, during which time she had had little control over the movements of her legs and arms, she decided it was time to go. As she pushed her way to the door, she passed a fashion editor who was discussing animatedly with her assistant which of the new designs they should choose to be photographed for a double-page spread in their magazine.

She paused briefly to listen to their conversation because,

fretting as she was under the restrictions imposed on her by the standstill policies of Ellis Firse and his colleagues, she envied those two women their editorial freedom with all her heart.

She caught the bus back to her office. It moved slowly and was brought to frequent halts by the traffic which built up into a solid, harassing block all the way. She had plenty of time to let her eyes linger lovingly on the great park they were passing. The grass, surprisingly green in spite of the dust-laden atmosphere of the heart of London, the brilliant colours of the flowers whose rich scents she longed to smell, brought back with a poignancy that was like a pain, the meadows and woods she had left behind.

She was swept by a desire to get away from the pressures of the life she had chosen, from the traffic fumes and the great soulless buildings, from the stress of too many people in too small a space, and return to the tranquillity of her home surroundings.

But she knew it was a feeling that had to be suppressed, at least for the time being. She could not give up now. It was not in her nature to resist a challenge, and that was what her new job undoubtedly was—a challenge to meet and master.

She was still fretting about those two journalists and their double-page spread when she stepped off the bus. She entered the building warily, as she always did, afraid of meeting the man she had been avoiding all the week, and dived towards the lift.

She put her finger on the call button and kept it there. She willed it to hurry. The man was all over the place and might turn up anywhere at any time. Her luck was clearly out this time. The lift was at the top floor. Her fingertip turned white with the pressure she was exerting on the button.

'It won't make the lift come any quicker, so I should ease off if I were you,' an amused voice said at her side.

He was there and she couldn't escape. She could not

bring herself to look at him. Instead she concentrated on the floor indicator over the lift doors. At last it arrived and they got in. They were alone. Her eyes were drawn involuntarily to his and he was smiling, but it was a mocking smile and it infuriated her.

'Busy?' he asked, with a hint of irony as if he thought the word could never be applied to her.

'Very,' she answered, wishing the ninth floor did not seem half-way to the sky. She eyed him suspiciously. Where was he going? To the ninth floor, too? To 'watch' her, as Janice Smythe, the ex-editor, had warned her he would do? But he left the lift at the eighth floor and she sagged with relief.

That afternoon an idea came to her—an incredible, impossible idea, and it made her heart thud to think of it, but after turning it over in her mind she became determined to follow it through. She kept it strictly to herself—after all, it might come to nothing.

Next morning, as soon as she arrived, she dialled Ellis Firse's extension. No, sorry, Mr. Firse was not in yet. Could she ring again? Cleone thought sourly that his secretary ought to tape that message and play it back continuously. Was the man never in?

Ten minutes later her phone rang. 'Miss Aston? Ellis Firse here. I understand you wanted me.'

Caught off guard, with her well-prepared speech gone right out of her head, she fumbled about in her brain for something to say until she could gather her wits—and her courage. 'I—well, yes, I . . .'

There was a long-suffering sigh from the other end and, afraid that he would ring off, she plunged straight in. 'Mr. Firse, would you—are you booked for lunch today?'

'Er—no, I don't think so.' He must have consulted his desk diary. 'No, I'm not. Why?'

'Well, I—may I—I mean, would you come out to lunch with me?'

There was a long silence, broken only by a lot of deep

breaths. At last he seemed to have recovered sufficiently to speak.

'Am I to take it that *you* are inviting *me* out to lunch?'

'Yes, Mr. Firse.' Her voice came out as a breathy squeak. She added hurriedly, 'It's a business lunch, a working lunch?'

'Is it now? For a moment you had me worried. And who, may I ask, is—to put it in strictly business terms—going to be financially responsible for this strictly business outing?'

'You mean who's going to pay? I am, of course.'

'May I ask where we would be having this—er—working lunch?'

'I'm sorry, but it's a secret.'

There was another silence, so long it unnerved her. What was he doing, searching madly for an excuse?

Grimly she pressed her lips together. She'd save him the trouble. 'It doesn't matter, Mr. Firse. It was just an idea . . .'

'Yes, Miss Aston, I accept your invitation. I shall have lunch—a business lunch—with you. If you'll come to my office about twelve-thirty——'

And twelve-thirty it was when she raised her hand to tap on the door which displayed the title 'Secretary—Managing Director'. Those three words fixed her to the spot as surely as if she were an ancient tree with multiple roots. She had invited the Managing Director to have lunch with her! Had she gone mad? How could she get out of it?

She knocked without being conscious of having done so and a pleasant voice called, 'Come in,' so in she went. Ellis Firse's secretary was young and pretty. She rose, her hand extended.

'You're Miss Aston, aren't you? I'm Carol Fisher. Mr. Firse is on the phone. He won't be long. Do sit down.'

Cleone was glad to rest her legs as they had become oddly weak. 'I've often spoken to you on the phone, haven't I?' she said. 'You always sound so cheerful. How do you manage it?'

Carol laughed. 'Probably because I'm happy in my job.

Mr. Firse is wonderful to work for. He's very considerate—you know, he's got the human touch!'

Was this another of his legion of girl-friends? Cleone wondered cynically. No, she couldn't be—she was wearing an engagement ring.

'I like your trousers, Miss Aston,' Carol commented, eyeing them enviously. 'What a lovely colour—a sort of violet, aren't they? Where did you buy them?'

'I didn't. I made them myself. The material's crushed velvet——'

'You made them? But they're so expertly cut, you wouldn't have guessed!'

'It's a hobby of mine,' Cleone said modestly. 'I took lessons in dressmaking and tailoring at the local technical college and it helped me enormously. I usually design my own things.'

Carol's eyes opened even wider. Ellis walked in. 'Mr. Firse, did you know you have an embryo *couture* designer on your staff? She designs her own clothes. She'd have a lot in common with your father, wouldn't she?'

Ellis burst into sardonic laughter at his secretary's ingenuous remark. 'That's rich,' he said. 'If you could have heard some of the things this girl's said about him. . . .'

'That's not true, Mr. Firse,' Cleone defended herself indignantly. 'It was his work I was talking about, not your father personally.'

'That's even better,' he laughed. 'Country kitten criticises internationally known *couturier*.'

'Country kitten!' It was almost a term of endearment, of familiarity. Cleone looked uncomfortably at Carol, wondering how she would take it, but she didn't appear to have noticed anything unusual. She had no doubt learned to be discreet, being the secretary of a man with a reputation for selecting and collecting women.

'Come into my office, puss.' He was carrying the metaphor through to its inevitable conclusion and it embarrassed her intensely.

He seemed happy. He had dropped all barriers and had obviously made up his mind to enjoy himself. 'Well,' she thought, 'he'll be seeing how the other half lives today, whether he wants to or not.'

Now it was his turn to eye her clothes. 'We're not going to the Hilton, that's plain. You—er—designed those velvet things you've got on your legs?'

'Yes, and made them.'

'M'm. With a little persuasion, my father might even take you on as an assistant designer. You'd love that, wouldn't you?' His voice was heavy with sarcasm. 'The only trouble is that you'd have to spend your time at first running his errands and learning to salaam at the great man's feet, after making a vow never to utter a word of criticism in his presence.'

Cleone smiled and looked round the room, admiring the expensive carpeting, the furniture, the décor.

The phone rang. 'Damn,' said Ellis, and lifted the receiver. 'Firse here. Oh, Maria.' His voice softened and he swung from side to side in his chair. 'Sorry, sweetie, can't be done.'

Cleone walked to the window. 'Sweetie' he called the girl on the phone. Annabelle was 'sweetie', Maria was 'sweetie'. Was it a sort of status term he gave to all his girlfriends, to distinguish them from the Miss Astons of this world, and all those strictly outside his circle—both social and amorous?

This was an awful room, she decided. The carpet was blue and she hated it. The decorations garish, the view terrible. How had she ever thought she liked it?

She walked back to her seat. He was staring at a blank page in his desk diary. 'I told you, sweetie, I'm booked solid the whole day, *and* the next, too. No,' his eyes moved to another empty page. 'That's out. Look, I'll ring you as soon as I've got a date free. All right?'

Cleone smiled without humour. 'Don't ring me, I'll ring you.' So that was his technique. She vowed silently that she would never give him the chance to give her the brush-off like that. She had too much pride.

He put the phone down and ran his finger round his collar. 'My word, that was a close thing!' he grinned. 'And it's all very well for you to smile, young Cleone.' There it was again, her name on his lips. 'But you don't have this trouble.'

'You shouldn't be so attractive.' She caught her own voice speaking the words and stared at him aghast. 'I'm sorry.'

A flicker passed across his eyes and he regarded her thoughtfully.

She added hastily, 'I mean, of course, to other women.'

'I quite understand, Miss Aston. There's no need for you to fall over backwards excluding yourself from my list of admirers.'

They were enemies again, and the thought tormented her.

'Now, before we go, I insist on one thing. The cost of this jaunt goes down on your expenses sheet. Having got that settled, *how* do we go? In my car?'

'I was thinking of going by Underground train.'

He thought for a moment and stood up. 'Right, Underground train it is. Lead the way.' He followed her out of the building to the street. 'Are you going to tell me where we're going?'

'Not yet,' she said, and he shrugged as if absolving himself of all responsibility.

They sat side by side in the train and as she watched their reflections in the tunnel-darkness beyond the windows, she could not believe that they were going out together. It was like a dream, and she knew that before long, she would have to wake up. He seemed content to be sitting there, his arm pressed against hers, as if they had known each other for years. Somehow it seemed right to be sitting beside him...

They changed trains and arrived at last at their journey's

end. They passed through the department store, up the stairs, over the soft carpets and came to a halt outside two swing doors. Ellis peered through the glass into the dimness beyond.

'Good grief,' he muttered, 'has there been a power cut?' His hand rested on her arm, restraining her. 'Where are you taking me, young woman? I insist on knowing before we go another step.'

'I'm going to show you the other side of fashion,' she said. 'This is a boutique. Have you ever been in one before?'

'No, I have not!'

'Well, you're going in one now.'

He seemed bewildered. 'But what about the lunch?'

'In there.' She went through the doors, hoping he would follow. He caught up with her in the semi-darkness.

'If you'd warned me, I'd have brought a torch,' he said into her ear, 'and ear-plugs.'

'I'm sorry about the noise,' she said, raising her voice so that he could hear, 'but this music goes on all the time. After a while you get used to it and don't even notice.'

He clapped his hand to his head. 'Its aim is no doubt to dull your critical faculties so that you stop being selective and accept without question whatever they choose to put under your nose.'

She shook her head pityingly and beckoned to him to follow her round the racks crammed with clothes. She lifted out one item after another, showing him the garments, pointing out the features of their design, the brilliantly matched colours, the fur linings, the feather scarves, the suede jackets and skirts. All the time the background music persisted. Flashing coloured lights swept high and low, playing over the clothes and subtly transforming their colours. They moved on to the accessories stands, looking at the belts, inches wide, studded, buckled and fringed.

There were gift tables spread with ornaments of bizarre design. There was a shoe department set in an alcove bounded by shining aluminium walls. Above their heads, brooding over everything, over the colour, the chatter of excited customers and the loud rhythmic beat of the music, was a deep blue ceiling with recessed lights which seemed curiously to emphasise the gloom.

He caught her arm. 'Feed me, woman,' he muttered in her ear. 'I'm exhausted. What are you aiming to do—torture me until I cry out for mercy and give in to all your demands?'

'Yes, something like that,' she said, and cowered away as he pretended to throttle her. The action did not seem remarkable—in such surroundings anything could happen.

She led the way to the food bar, and even there the dimness persisted, despite the moving lights which flashed and merged into subtle, exciting shades and shadows.

'What will you have to eat, Mr. Firse?'

'You choose.'

'Sandwiches and coffee?' He nodded. 'If you'll find a seat, I'll get them.'

Obediently he collapsed his length on to a low bench seat with a high shielding back and waited patiently while she collected the food and carried it across on a tray.

He helped her unload it and shifted along the seat so that she could move in beside him. Contentedly and in complete accord, they ate their sandwiches. They were drinking their coffee when she said, apologetically, 'I'm afraid these surroundings are very different from those you're used to at lunch-time.'

He turned sideways so that he could look at her. 'And what am I used to at lunch-time?'

'Oh,' she said expansively, 'a hotel with waiter-service, a four-course meal, wine . . .'

He moved nearer. 'I'll tell you a secret. I'll make a confession. Every lunch-time, when I haven't got a working lunch—such as this,' he smiled provocatively, 'I send my secretary round to the local pub for some sandwiches. Then, before she goes to her lunch, she makes me some coffee. So I eat alone—quite simply—in peace and quiet. Disappointed?'

'No, only surprised.' She added shyly, 'And pleased.'

'Thanks,' he said. 'That certainly is something, coming from my sternest critic.'

He said, after a while, 'I've come to the conclusion that it's the generation gap that's the trouble. We see this sort of thing from different angles. I'm too old.'

'But you're surely not much older than I am!'

'Thanks for flattering me. In fact, I'm thirty-two, nine years older than you are. Nine years makes quite a difference, you know.'

'Mr. Firse?' Now she would take the risk. 'What did you think of the clothes?'

There was a long pause. 'I suppose you want me to say I liked them?'

She was on the defensive at once. 'But this is fashion, real fashion.'

'The real thing, of course.' He was being sarcastic and she rounded on him.

'Of course it is. It's fashion that's alive, it's got vitality and meaning. It's tuned in to the needs of young people, it reflects their ways of living and their thinking. And what's more, it's within their reach, financially and physically—they can come to these places and touch it, feel it, try it on. It isn't locked away, out of reach, with "touch me not" written all over it.'

'You wouldn't be getting at my father?'

'I'm sorry if I'm upsetting you, but——' How could she reach him? 'Can't you *feel* it? Isn't there something here that makes you respond to it, an urgency, a sense of change, of new ideas? *I* can feel it. The designers of these clothes have broken through the barriers which people like your father have been imposing on dress design for years. There's originality here, a sort of trying-out, an experimental mood...' She ran out of words.

'Yes, I was wondering when you were going to stop.

Don't push your product too hard, Cleone. It gives a bad impression and leaves an unpleasant taste.'

She grew angry. 'Can't you see what I'm trying to say?' Even in the dimness he could see the tears glittering.

'My sweet Cleone, don't give me the hard-sell. I'm immune to it. I get it so often. Let me relax and absorb. Let me see for myself and form my own judgment.' She was silent. He went on, 'My dear wide-eyed innocent, look at it another way. Stop being so ingenuous and be a little cynical. Why do you think so much effort is being made to satisfy the requirements of the young these days? Because they are the people with the money, the spending power——'

'I *know* that,' she interrupted edgily, 'but——'

'Therefore,' he went on, 'their whims and fancies are pandered to, in order—to put it earthily—to rake in the cash. This stuff,' he indicated the racks of clothes with a brief wave of his hand, 'mass-produced and mass-marketed as it is, is the uniform of the young. It reduces them all to one level. This is conformity with a capital "C". There's no expression of individual personalities here. They're all ironed out flat by the calculated sameness of these clothes. Now, in *couture*, there *is* individuality and originality, on a much higher plane.'

'At a price,' she said, 'at an enormous price.'

'Agreed, at a price. But many people think it's worth paying that price just to be a little different.'

'But the number of people who can afford to pay so much for a dress or a coat—hundreds of pounds sometimes—is shrinking fast. And even those left must surely think twice before parting with so much money, because they must realise that we're living in an age of throw-away clothes. Fashions change so fast these days that even they wouldn't want to be lumbered with a white elephant that cost them a fortune to buy. Anyway, the idea of the wealthy woman spending her mornings at her *couturiers*, because she has nothing better to do, being fitted for fabulous and costly clothes which she wears once, then hands on to her servants, is too feudal and out-of-date for words. The fashion world is more democratic nowadays, more within the reach of the ordinary person. And the whole structure of society is changing. Fashion must respond to those changes, or die.'

He smiled and the look in his eyes subtly changed the subject. 'Don't get political,' he said softly. 'I'm not in the mood for that.' He said, still looking at her, 'This atmosphere, these lighting effects, the semi-darkness, this base-boosted music with its persistent, primitive drum-beat—it all appeals to one thing—the most basic of all instincts. To put it in equally basic language, it's sexy.' His eyes lingered lazily on her white ribbed cotton blouse stretched tightly over her breasts, took in her clinging velvet slacks.

'Like you are,' he whispered, and saw the colour creeping into her cheeks. 'Has no one ever told you? What is Ivor thinking of? He must be only half a man.' His hand moved towards her. He pulled it back and pushed it into his pocket. 'We'd better go, otherwise I might start making love to you, and that would be shocking! Quite the wrong time of day.'

He smiled and she smiled back. 'If I told him what I was thinking,' she mused, 'if I said, "I want you to make love to me because I love you," what would he do?'

She searched feverishly for her handbag and led the way to the door.

In the daylight they blinked like two people who had awakened from a long and pleasant dream.

'We'll take a taxi back,' he said. When she protested that it was a long way, he merely remarked, 'No arguments. It's on the firm.'

In the taxi, she strained away into the corner. He seemed to have the same idea and hugged his corner, too. Now they had returned to normality, the situation between them had changed radically. They had nothing to say to each other.

Cleone was thinking, 'The whole thing's been a fiasco. I should never have suggested it. It's made no difference whatever to his attitude.'

'Is Maria a model, Mr. Firse?'

He turned from the window and frowned. 'I'm sorry, I didn't hear. I was miles away.'

She repeated her question.

'Yes, Maria's a model. She works for my father, too.'

'What happens when Annabelle and Maria are there together and you arrive?'

He laughed shortly. 'The situation is delicate.'

'Are all your girl-friends models?'

'No, not all of them. Anyway,' he asked curtly, 'why this sudden interest in my private life? I don't pry into yours.'

She rubbed her cheek as though he had slapped it. 'I'm sorry.' She stared miserably out of the window.

He stirred after a while. 'My father would like to see you. He has a favour to ask of you. He has a—difficult client. She hates fitting sessions, apparently, and just doesn't turn up when asked.'

He looked her over. 'My father says you're so like her in height and shape that the fittings could be done on you—if you were willing.'

'Oh. But I don't really think . . .'

'Look, I played along with you this morning. I gave you my time—which is precious—and my attention. I needn't have done. I could have turned your suggestion down flat.'

That was a subtle way of reminding her, she realised, in case she had forgotten, of his exalted position. And a clever way of putting on the pressure. It could even be called blackmail. Nevertheless, she knew she had to agree.

'When does he want to see me?'

'This evening? About seven?'

She nodded.

'Thanks,' he said, and sank back into his corner.

She was bewildered by the alteration in his mood. What had she done to make him change it so drastically? Now they were nearing their journey's end and she had made no progress at all with her case for greater editorial freedom.

She would have to go back to the others and report total failure. She couldn't let them down like that.

'Mr. Firse?'

'Yes?' He wouldn't even look at her now.

'Am I—am I going to be allowed to make changes in the magazine?' He moved impatiently. 'The object of my invitation today was to show you the other side of the coin——'

'I'm aware of that.'

'—to prove to you that these days fashion is not just *couture* calling the tune. Once *haute couture* was so influential that it used to push its way downwards through all the other layers of the fashion scene. Now the pressure is in the other direction. Fashion is really a bit like a river, and the styles you've seen today are all the tributaries running into it, feeding it and making it flow faster.' She paused to take stock of her progress, looking into his face and trying to calculate the effect on him of her oratory. His expression gave nothing away.

She went on, desperate now, 'If fashion reflects the times—as it always does, you've only got to look at the history books to prove that fact—then fashion magazines should reflect those times, too, otherwise they die.'

He still did not answer and this time she panicked.

'Mr. Firse,' she paused to make him look at her, 'when you appointed me to this job, it must have meant that you had faith in me. Can't you follow up that faith by trusting me and giving me more freedom to do that job as I think it should be done?'

His laughter broke the tense silence, and it was laughter of capitulation as well as exasperation. 'I must hand it to you, young Cleone, if there's one thing you've got in good measure it's persistence and tenacity. You just don't give in, do you?'

He leaned across and took her hand, but dropped it after a few seconds. 'All I can promise you is this. Since it's a matter of policy, the management is involved and it would have to be discussed by them. If necessary, would you be prepared to come along and support your case?'

'Yes, if you think it would do any good.'

'Do any good? Good grief, once you get going on them, they won't stand a chance. Your eloquence is such that it would move Everest!'

They were back at the office. He paid the taxi fare and they walked together into the building. They paused outside his room.

'Thank you for coming with me today, Mr. Firse. I hope you enjoyed it.'

'Enjoyed it, Miss Aston? I——' He stopped and continued in a flat tone, 'Yes, I enjoyed it, thanks.'

He went into his room and closed the door.

CHAPTER V

It was just after seven when Cleone pressed the bell at the entrance to the Firse residence. It had been a problem choosing what to wear. In the end she had picked out two things she had made herself—the white long-sleeved blouse and a black skirt cleverly cut to swing into a flare towards the hemline.

Ellis opened the door. 'Nice of you to come,' he said impersonally. 'I'm to take you straight to the fitting room.'

Without another word he took her coat and led the way. As usual, she followed a few steps behind him. François was there and his greeting was as stiff and formal as before. Ellis did not leave. Instead, he picked up a magazine and flipped through it disinterestedly.

'My son has explained the position?' François asked. He studied her with a professional, assessing eye. 'You are so like my client in build that it is quite astonishing.' He seemed to notice her clothes. 'My son tells me you are an embryo designer.'

Was that an attempt at a joke? Cleone could not tell from his face, but in a way she hoped it was, because it would mean he was warming to her just a little.

She shook her head modestly. 'I just buy material that appeals to me and—well, think about it. Then I——' She shrugged, trying to say that what she did was too unprofessional to talk about, 'cut it out and try it on.'

His nod was approving. 'I am familiar with that process. That is how an idea is born sometimes. The fabric suggests it, perhaps . . .'

'Oh, but,' she protested, 'I wouldn't call what I buy "fabric". It's ordinary material that I get in sales or—or in the market.'

She flushed and looked uncertainly at Ellis, who did not appear to be listening.

François nodded again. 'There's nothing wrong with that. But you would find better quality fabric easier to handle, more responsive.'

'I know,' she replied, 'but I've never been able to afford to pay much.'

'Then you are all the more clever to get such good results with what you do buy.' The compliment came softly and sincerely from the great designer and brought a delighted glow to her cheeks.

She looked at the designer's son who had found a chair and seemed prepared to sit the fitting out. He was still looking at the magazine.

'Do you ever draw a sketch of what you are aiming at?' François asked. 'No? I think you might find it easier if you did. Would you like to see some of my sketches from past collections?'

He went into an adjoining room and returned with a handful of drawings which he spread out on a bench. 'These ideas come to me at all times,' he explained. 'I may be eating or reading, or out walking or even in the bath!' He smiled at her for the first time and she caught her breath. She was aware that she had stumbled upon the fount of warmth and humanity in him which his son, close as he was in relationship, had failed to find. Because of her interest in his subject, she had been privileged to share for one moment the intimacy of his inspiration and his passionate absorption with his life's work.

She studied the sketches and found that although many of them appeared to be of the same dress, minute details had been altered, changing completely the line of the garment and its ultimate effect.

'After the final sketches,' François was explaining, 'come the *toiles*. The model girls show them to me and those I approve are made at last into the actual garments in the chosen fabrics. Then of course accessories have to be selected with great care—shoes, hats, gloves and so on. As you can see,' he smiled again, 'it all involves a great deal of work and much apparent chaos. We all go a little mad as collection time approaches, we become irritable, our nerves are frayed—but the result is triumph and much personal satisfaction for all of us involved.'

He looked at Ellis, who had found another magazine, and that seemed to remind him of the object of her visit. 'Now I think it's time for the gown to be brought in. I'll call my fitter. She has stayed on especially to do it.'

The woman was not young and she came in with a slightly harassed air and eyed Cleone with that same professional eye. 'Remarkable,' she commented, 'the shape, the height.'

Her name, she told Cleone, was really Jean. 'But Monsieur François,' she smiled at him, 'insists on calling me Jeanne, pronounced the French way. Are you ready, Miss Aston?' She held up the dress, which appeared to be a long evening gown.

Cleone looked round for somewhere to change, but it seemed that she was not expected to be so shy. Since she was not a hardened professional model, accustomed to trying on dresses in front of strangers, she hesitated. She wouldn't have minded François staying—he, in fact, had left the room, but Ellis . . .

He saw her looking at him and smiled mockingly. 'What's the matter? You don't surely want me to leave my comfortable corner, just so that you can try on a dress?' He settled himself down more comfortably. 'I won't look.'

And she had to be satisfied with that. She remembered that he was used to seeing half-clad models—he even took them in his arms to comfort them sometimes, as she had seen for herself. What would happen if she started crying? she wondered as she turned her back on him and unbuttoned her blouse and stepped out of her skirt. He would no doubt laugh and tell her to snap out of it.

With the fitter's help, she got into the dress. It cascaded over her shoulders and the skirt slipped down to her ankles. The colour was cerise and the full flowing lines of the skirt delighted the dressmaker in her. From shoulder to waist, wide bands of the material were gathered into soft folds across the bodice and interwoven diagonally one with the other. The back dropped to well below the shoulder blades. The fabric was silk and felt indescribably soft to the touch.

The fitter purred with satisfaction, making only a few alterations.

'I'll get Monsieur François,' she muttered, and left the room.

Ellis put down his magazine and rose lazily. He moved behind her as she gazed at herself in the long mirror. His fingers closed round her bare arms and he contemplated her reflection.

'Well, Cleone,' he said softly, 'this is *couture*.' He lifted a fold of the material. 'This is the *real thing*. Nothing synthetic about it, nothing artificial. Hand-made mostly, too. Doesn't it appeal to you, purist that you are?'

She didn't answer. What could she say?

'Remember the clothes we saw this morning? Remember how they hung, rack after rack, in sets of ten or twenty? Remember the fabrics they were made of? Imitation this, imitation that? What price the real thing now?'

Her colour rose with her temper and she shook off his tormenting hands. 'It's quite impossible to compare them. They're two entirely different things. It's like comparing a purse with a suitcase—they're both made to contain objects, but they both exist for different purposes.'

He moved round in front of her, drawing out a cigarette and lighting it. 'M'm,' he mused, lounging against a table and eyeing her, 'rather like comparing two women—a mere girl-friend and the woman you're going to marry. They both exist for different purposes.' He grinned provocatively. 'When's the shoe coming my way?'

Somehow she managed to contain her temper. His father walked in.

'Ellis,' he said, 'Annabelle sends a message. She will be ready soon.'

Ellis nodded and found his magazine again. So that was why he was waiting, Cleone thought dully, to take his girl-friend out. She noticed, without much interest, that he was reading a copy of *Salon*.

François circled slowly round her. She could not tell from his expression whether he was pleased or dissatisfied. The fitter hovered in the background. Here and there he touched the dress and spoke to the woman, who responded immediately to his suggestions.

At last he said the fitting was over. The fitter helped Cleone to climb out of the dress and as she slipped on her blouse and pulled on her skirt, she hoped Ellis was too absorbed in his reading to notice.

François thanked her for coming. 'My client should be pleased with her dress.' He smiled. 'Did you approve of it, Miss Aston?'

'I thought it was beautiful.'

'In what way? How did you form your judgment?'

'Oh,' she shook her head, unable to explain, 'just the whole effect.'

'When you look at a dress,' he told her, 'you should try to understand the principle on which it is based. Why is it gathered or tucked or draped here, why is the fabric left alone there, to speak for itself? You should look at the accessories, the model's *coiffure*, and note how it blends with the dress. Why is she wearing that particular hat? You understand what I'm trying to say?'

'You mean that one shouldn't look at one particular part of an outfit in isolation from the rest?'

'Exactly. Neither should you isolate fashion itself from its surroundings. Women's fashions are only one small part of a continuous process of changing fashions. Other influences—the moral, social and political climate of the times—are at work all the time, affecting people's outlooks and ideas, and this in turn affects the clothes they wear.'

Cleone seized her chance. 'Mr. Firse,' she called him by his real name, but he did not seem to object, 'I understand what you're saying, but what I can't understand is why you haven't taken your own advice and opened a boutique like so many other *couturiers* have done. If you adapted your own designs, as they do, for the ready-to-wear market, your clothes would reach the ordinary person who can't afford to pay *couture* prices. It would also help you financially . . .'

'*Miss Aston!*' The astringent tones of Ellis Firse stopped her abruptly.

'I'm sorry.' She looked round for her coat. The sooner she escaped from the son's icy stare the better.

But, surprisingly, his father was not annoyed. 'Miss Aston,' his voice was quiet, but his eyes were shadowed with sadness, 'I know what you are trying to say. I'm aware that my craft is passing, as other great crafts have passed, into obscurity. I know that the creative gifts I possess will, before very long, be valueless and unrecognised. I'm also aware that times are changing and that time itself is going by.' He smiled. 'At my age, how could I not know it? It did not need an eager, attractive young woman to tell me that, although I'm sure you are convinced that I was fast aleep in an ivory tower until you came along to wake me up!'

'I'm sorry,' Cleone said again, feeling that the two words

were quite inadequate to erase her audacity from his mind.

The door opened. 'Ellis.' Annabelle was decorating the entrance, groomed to perfection, her smile Mona Lisa-like, the sunlight from the landing window casting round her an ethereal glow. She tensed, poised momentarily like a bird of prey, and swooped. Seconds later, his arms were round her.

'Ellis,' she whispered again, 'Ellis darling.' She held up her mouth. He lowered his head and kissed her—on the forehead.

Cleone felt sick with revulsion and jealousy. 'That's right, Ellis Firse,' she thought savagely, 'elusive as ever. Never commit yourself. Always compromise.'

She had to go. She searched for her handbag and found it.

François walked across to Annabelle. Automatically, she took up a model's pose and allowed him to inspect the suit she was wearing. It was pale blue, impeccably tailored and pure 'François' from collar to hem.

'Where are you taking her?' he asked his son.

Ellis named one of the most expensive hotels in London. And was it only a few hours ago, Cleone reflected, when he had sat beside her, eating sandwiches and drinking coffee in the semi-darkness of a boutique? And what had he said—that he'd enjoyed it? How he must have laughed about it afterwards with his secretary!

'That is excellent,' François was saying. 'She will be seen there by the maximum number of people. Be sure you sit in a prominent place, my dear Annabelle. And no running away by yourselves as you usually do!'

So she was modelling François outfits even in her leisure time—acting as a walking advertisement for his creations.

'Can I give you a lift, Miss Aston?' Ellis asked.

'No, thank you, Mr. Firse.' She made her face as expressionless as his. 'I prefer to go by bus.'

He shrugged, put his arm round Annabelle's waist and led her from the room.

Cleone gave a progress report next morning to her colleagues. She thought they would be encouraged by what she told them, but they shook their heads.

'You won't make them change their minds, Cleone,' Rick said. 'You might as well give up. We have. This has all been said before, and nothing has come of it.'

'I'm not the sort to give in easily, Rick. If they don't come round to our way of thinking soon, I'll take matters into my own hands, even if they threaten to sack me. I suggest we take a positive attitude—let's discuss the title of the new magazine!'

They laughed, but it was not long before there was a list of possible names in front of her. They decided provisionally on *Fashion Talk*, and Rick promised to make a few sketches of his ideas for the cover of the first issue. He said they were really building castles in the air, but they all seemed happier when they left her.

She began to dream of the new magazine which had started to take shape in her mind. She jotted down some ideas for editorials, considered introducing a beauty section and decided that even the advertising material would have to be revised.

The phone rang. 'Miss Aston?' He was as usual abrupt and businesslike. 'Are you busy?'

'Busy?' He had caught her off guard and his voice, as always, set her pulses racing. 'I—well, we—Yes, of *course* I'm busy!'

He laughed. 'Responsibilities of your position weighing you down, no doubt.' He seemed in a good mood. 'All high-powered executives should take time off now and then. Are you booked for this evening?'

She grew suspicious. 'Why?'

'I have an evening free. I should like to take you out to dinner.'

So he intended using her to fill a yawning gap in his engagement diary! 'He'll wine you and dine you,' Janice Smythe had said.

'I'm sorry, I'm booked. I—I have a date.'

'Oh.' There was a long pause. 'Is Ivor in town?'

'Ivor? No, he's not. I'm—going to a dance.'

'May I ask where? And with whom?' His voice sounded odd.

She did not reply.

He said, 'I'm coming up,' and the receiver crashed down.

Waiting for him, counting in her mind the number of floors he would have to pass in the lift, she clasped and unclasped her hands. Why should she tell him? Why should he be allowed to pry into her private life when he had snubbed her for doing the same to his?

He came in without knocking. Now her hands were clasped so tightly she wondered if she would ever get them apart again.

'You didn't answer my question.' It was a statement as cold as his eyes.

'I didn't have to,' she fenced. 'My private life is my own concern.'

'And what "private life",' he smeared the words with meaning, 'have you got that I don't know about?'

Again she retreated into silence.

'Look, Miss Aston, I brought you into this great big wicked world of London,' she heard the sarcastic inflection, 'I therefore feel a certain sense of responsibility towards you.'

'If you're worried about my morals, I can look after them myself, thank you.'

He made an exasperated sound. 'All I ask, Cleone,' his use of her name almost weakened her resolve, 'is an answer to my questions "Where?" and "With whom?" Then I'll go.'

Sulkily she told him where she was going. She added, keeping her eyes down, 'Alone.'

'Why?'

Still not looking at him, she told him how she had read

that all good fashion journalists should visit the dance halls if they wanted to see the true fashion of the day. So, being a good fashion journalist, she intended to do just that. She had looked through her local newspaper and had found a dance that was taking place that evening. 'And that's where I'm going,' she finished.

'She's so dedicated to her work, she's doing overtime.' Cleone looked up and found that he was smiling. 'You'll be asking for double pay soon.' He sat in the visitor's chair looking, for some reason, decidedly relieved.

She grinned at him. 'So my morals are safe. For the moment.'

He did not respond to the bait in her words. He said, 'You're not going alone. You've got yourself a partner. Me.'

'No, thank you. You wouldn't fit in, not where I'm going.'

'I take exception to that, Miss Aston. I could remind you of my position and reprimand you. But I won't. I'll pick you up at eight prompt.' He stood up and looked at her desk, noting the absence of clutter and its lack of anything that resembled work.

'As you said on the phone, you're *very* busy, aren't you?'

'Yes, I am, Mr. Firse. I've been thinking about the lay-out of the new magazine.' She smiled up at him impishly and he looked astonished.

'What new magazine?'

'The one that supersedes *Salon*. We've been discussing possible names and have temporarily decided on *Fashion Talk*.'

He walked towards her menacingly. 'If you aren't the most unscrupulous, artful, designing little minx I've ever come across . . .'

'But, Mr. Firse, I was only thinking.'

'*Your* thoughts, Miss Aston, are as dangerous as other men's deeds. As I've said to you before, if you put too much pressure on me, I'll go the other way to such an extent that you'll find yourself unemployed.'

'I'm sorry,' she said. She seemed to spend her time apologising to the Firse family. She swallowed. 'But you can't stop me dreaming.'

He went out.

'I'm not going there to dance,' she warned him when he called for her at her flat. 'Only as an observer.'

'Pure research,' he grinned, 'with an emphasis on the "pure".' He looked her over. 'House of Aston?' he enquired, eyebrows raised.

She nodded. 'Aston designed and created.' It was a simple blue and white dress with a scooped-out neckline and cut to fit her figure closely. 'I'm making another which I've adapted from one of your father's designs. I hope he won't mind.'

'He'll probably sue you for stealing his ideas.' He looked round the hall. 'If we weren't going places, I'd ask you to invite me in.'

'But you must have seen this flat before. Janice Smythe lived here.'

'What exactly are you implying?'

'Well,' she looked away uncomfortably, 'she told me you would "wine me and dine me" as she put it, so I assumed you had done the same to her. You seem to have so many women friends . . .'

'I think it's time we went.' He led the way to the car. It took them ten minutes to get there. He paid at the door and as they entered the dance hall, he put a hand to his head.

'The noise!' he groaned, but she could hardly hear him. 'It's the generation gap again. I'm too old.'

Looking round at the young people swaying and twisting and, it seemed, induced into a state of hypnosis by the repetitive, jarring dissonance of the music, Cleone felt that she was too old, too. But she had come to watch, not to participate.

They found a seat in a corner where the noise dwindled

to tolerable limits. But they could feel the vibration caused by the drums shaking the floor beneath their feet and moving upwards through the legs of the chairs. Because the seats had been pushed close together to give more space to the dancers, Ellis's shoulder pressed against hers. He turned his head and smiled.

She said, touching his arm, 'You see how informal their clothes are? No one dresses up these days, not even for dances. You see how appropriate the fashions in that boutique were? They were made for the times because they grew out of the needs of the times.'

'Yes, teacher,' he said meekly. 'But,' he countered, 'the world doesn't only consist of young people. There are the middle-aged and elderly still around, not to mention the in-betweens, like me. Can you imagine me wearing those clothes?'

Cleone laughed with him. 'But older people would go to their favourite shop or store and find things to suit them there. You see, Mr. Firse,' she looked at him with concentrated earnestness, '*couture* doesn't come into ordinary everyday life.'

He bent down and whispered, 'Are you trying the hard sell again, young Cleone? Because, if so, I'll . . .'

'I'm sorry, Mr. Firse,' she said wearily.

He lifted her hand on to his knee and covered it with his own. 'And will you stop Mr. Firse-ing me? In such surroundings and in such company, it's not only feudal, as you would put it, but almost indecent. Call me Ellis, for God's sake. Go on.'

'Yes, Ellis.'

'That's much better,' he said.

The lights were dimmed, the music became soft and sweet. The singer sang a love song. The dancers moved slowly, intimately close. The mood caught them both and Cleone found herself on her feet and in his arms dancing as closely to her partner as all the others around them.

His cheek found hers and she wanted the moment to

crystallise and remain unchanged for ever. But time moved on, the music ended, the dancers dispersed. He led her back to their seats, his hand holding hers, and he did not release it even when they sat down.

Had he held Annabelle's hand, Cleone wondered, last night when they'd dined together? Did he dance with all his girl-friends as intimately as he had just danced with her?

He whispered, 'I'm sorry, I couldn't resist the music. It was a case of pure research being put to a practical test.'

'Did you learn anything from it?'

'It will take time for the results to be known,' he answered, smiling. Then he grew restless. 'I could do with a drink, and I don't mean the sort of stuff they serve here. I mean my own. Have you seen enough?'

'I think so,' she said, wishing she knew what he meant. Was this the end of their evening together?

But he did not take her home. He pulled up outside his own flat. 'Will you come in?'

She stiffened. 'I—don't think so, thanks, Ellis.'

'What are you afraid of?' He seemed genuinely surprised. 'That I'll seduce you? I've never yet been known to do that to an unwilling woman. And from the sound of it, rape simply isn't worth the effort. So, to paraphrase the words of an obsequious salesman, "assuring you of my best intentions at all times," will you come into my parlour?'

'As the spider said to the fly,' she laughed, then she saw his steadfast gaze and nodded.

'Make yourself at home,' Ellis said, showing her into the living area of his flat.

She caught her breath and looked round in disbelief. All this for one man—this luxury, this floor space, this colour and quality! 'Make myself at home?' she thought. There was nothing homely about this stage setting, this background of beauty without feeling, this atmosphere of austere touch-me-not orderliness.

The couch and chairs were covered in patterned silk

damask. The coffee table, placed centrally, was round and white and supported on a 'stalk' and reminded her of a mushroom. In isolated splendour in the grate was an electric imitation log fire. The pile of the biscuit-coloured carpet curled and sprang and invited bare toes to curl up in it. But no bare toes could surely have ever been allowed to walk there. Imitation flowers were arranged in an expensive-looking vase.

She looked at the books around the walls, half expecting them to be imitation, too. She thought, with pity, 'Is this his home? Is this where he spends his hours away from the office, in these barren, cold, theatrical surroundings?'

He was watching her face. 'What's the matter—don't you like my home?' There was a sharpness in his voice.

'It's beautiful, Ellis,' she managed quickly, and sat down, stiff with unease.

He sat beside her. 'But it's not the real thing, is that it? To you, it's not "home"—just a collection of inanimate objects, with no one to breathe life and meaning into them?'

She sat forward uncomfortably, wishing she hadn't come. Pity for him stirred within her, pity for this rich man who had everything he wanted—even women at his beck and call. A luxurious flat, but no place he could truly call a home.

'Drink, Cleone?'

'Please, Ellis.' Her parched throat cried out for liquid.

He put a glass in her hand. She drank and immediately her throat was on fire. He sat opposite her and started on a cigarette.

'For heaven's sake, relax,' he said, but there was an edginess about him too.

She finished her drink and he pressed another into her hand. She accepted it because she needed something to steady her nerves. He was watching her through the smoke screen he had created around himself. To escape from those searching eyes, she rose and inspected the bookshelves, but his eyes followed her even there.

As she sat down, she commented on the 'learnedness' of his books and he laughed.

'Did you think I was an ignoramus? You'll no doubt be surprised to hear that I'm a graduate. Sit back, my dear Cleone, and prepare to be entertained. I'll give you a résumé of my career.' He drew on his cigarette and half closed his eyes in the effort of remembering. 'Er—a long way back, private school—I was coddled there. No rough and tumble of the local primary school for me. Then public school, one of the famous ones—yes, I expected that nose to be lifted in horror! There I was taught my rightful place in life—socially, in the top class, of course, but intellectually? That didn't matter as much as one's status. Ability wasn't so highly valued. After that, university. . . .'

'Oxford?' Cleone asked.

'But of course, Oxford,' he replied with cynicism. 'Where else? Then followed a short spell in art—my father hoped to bring to light some latent artistic talent. But alas, such talents were so latent they didn't exist.' He tapped the ash from his cigarette. 'I should have been an engineer, but my father was horrified when I suggested it, equating it with dirtying one's hands. So that was out. Now tell me about yourself.'

'Sorry. After that, I pass.'

He leaned forward. 'Tell me. I told you. Fair's fair.'

'Well,' she sipped her drink, 'ordinary education, primary and secondary schools. I passed all my exams. Then journalism, local paper stuff. Socially and pedigree-wise, I simply don't quality to be put on your list of girl-friends.'

'Who said I wanted to put you on my list of girl-friends?'

She moved her fingers restlessly round the stem of her wine glass. A door had just slammed shut in her face. 'Forgive me for trespassing,' she said heavily.

He moved to sit beside her and she stiffened again. 'You know my father will be showing his collection soon? You'll be invited, of course, together with the rest of the press. But the buyers are of paramount importance. They're treated like queens. They represent hard cash, because their selection or rejection can make or break a *couturier.*' He got himself another drink and resumed his seat beside her. 'During the preparations for the showing, I don't go near the place. The chaos and noise should be seen to be believed.' He stubbed out his cigarette and started on another. He seemed to be chain-smoking, and the smell of the atmosphere almost choked her.

She looked round, desperately seeking a means of escape like a handcuffed prisoner in court. He watched her every movement steadily, unflinchingly, as a marksman watches, with raised rifle, the evasive, tortuous flight of a bird he has caught in his sights.

She felt a sudden longing to see her parents' home, to feel the warmth of their welcome, to see the old, well-worn furniture and walk in her own rather shabby bedroom.

'I'm going home soon,' she told him, surprising herself with her own decision.

'Missing Ivor?' he asked casually.

'Ivor?' She looked at him sharply. Suppose she told him she hadn't thought of Ivor until he mentioned his name? 'Yes, very much.'

'Still saving up for that house?'

'Of course. We'll probably discuss it at the weekend.'

He stubbed out his cigarette. 'I'll take you home.'

She followed him into the hall and he helped her with her coat. His hands rested on her shoulders and he turned her round.

He smiled. 'Have you learned anything from your evening of overtime?'

She nodded. His face was so near, too near for comfort. 'Thank you for coming with me and being my partner.'

She had known all along that it was inevitable, that he would expect a goodnight kiss, the sort of kiss he had given Annabelle, a peck on the forehead. But his mouth went homing to hers and she did not expect the lingering, engulfing, lover-like kiss that was, in its urgency, almost a gesture of farewell.

He let her go at last and she groped unsteadily towards the wall, seeking support. After that, there was nothing more to say and he took her home in silence. She thanked him again. He answered with a nod and a brief smile and drove away.

CHAPTER VI

CLEONE called her colleagues in to her room to discuss an editorial she had written. She intended using it in the next edition of *Salon*. It was a thought-provoking piece of writing and a complete breakaway from the usual stilted paragraphs of 'pure jargon', as Cleone called it, which until now had passed for editorials in that magazine. As it stood, it was also a challenge to the management, and for that reason she wanted to test her colleagues' reactions to it.

She intended it to act, she told them, as a scene-setter for what was to come—she was quite positive about it—a new-style publication aimed at the younger age groups.

'Made any progress yet?' Ben asked. 'Because if you have, let me know, won't you, so that I can get going on some fresh-angle advertising. We don't want to be stuck with the dowdy old-style stuff in a brand-new magazine.'

'Unfortunately, Ben, there's nothing to report—yet. Every time I raise the subject with Mr. Firse, I feel I'm like the proverbial irresistible force up against an immovable object. Incidentally,' she said, 'keep quiet about this editorial I've written. I won't be happy until it's safely at the printers. It's vital that it goes in, because it will help to prepare the way for the new publication, condition the readers, if you like, into accepting the changeover. I'm going home this evening until Monday. When I get back,

I'll tackle Mr. Firse again.'

Rick grinned, 'He'll get fed up with you.'

'That's probably the idea, isn't it?' laughed Sarah. 'Wear him down until he gives in!'

'The old drops of water on a stone technique,' Joanna commented. 'The only trouble is, that way we could all be dead before he changes his mind!'

As they were leaving, Joanna pointed at Cleone's desk. 'It looks as if you're setting up a bring-and-buy stall. What are you going to do with all those accessories?'

'Wear them,' Cleone joked, picking up a glittering imitation coronet and setting it on her hair.

'I like this hair-piece,' Joanna said, trying without success to fix it to her hair. 'I suppose all these are for photographs?' She looked at the black shoes. 'Those are fab. Can I try them on?'

'Better not. They're only to be used by the model and then returned to the wholesaler. D'you like this belt? The manufacturer's public relations girl brought it in to show me. Asked if I could feature it in an article in the magazine.' She made a face. 'In this set-up, I'd probably have to ask the managing director for permission before I could do that!'

Joanna went out and passed a tall, slender girl hovering outside. Cleone invited her in, thinking that, with her poise and her good looks, she must surely be a model.

The girl introduced herself. 'Denise Mitcham from the François set-up. I understand I've got a photographic session for *Salon* this afternoon.'

'That's right.' Cleone opened the door of one of the long wall cupboards and took out a suitcase. 'The clothes are all in here, all François designs, of course. We're not allowed to feature anything else.' She smiled ruefully. 'Beautiful though they are, it gets a bit monotonous.'

The girl turned as the door opened. 'Hallo, Ellis,' Denise said, going up to him and touching his shoulder with a playful gesture. 'Quite a stranger!'

'Hallo, Denise.' He was off-hand. 'I've been busy lately. Sorry.'

She pouted. 'I understand, darling. You don't love me any more.' She patted him again, picked up the suitcase and left.

Cleone fiddled with her notebook. Another one from his harem, she was thinking. He must surely be the most chased-after man in London. Then she spotted the editorial she had been working on and managed to slide another piece of paper over it.

'Take that thing off.'

She jumped violently at the curt order, thinking he had seen her action. 'What thing?'

He nodded towards her head and she raised her hand to feel the coronet she had forgotten to remove.

'It's artificial.' He went on sarcastically, 'I'd have thought that a connoisseur of the real thing such as you claim to be would have recognised it as such. In any case, it hardly enhances the looks of a country kitten.'

Annoyed with him for reducing her to size, she pulled it from the tangle of her curls and put it down. He sat on a corner of her desk. 'Today's the day, isn't it, when the prodigal daughter returns home? Which train are you catching?'

She told him. 'I'm leaving half an hour early. Do you mind?'

'I doubt if I shall remove you from your job just for that.' He smiled. 'But mind you're in on time on Monday morning!' He picked up a paper clip and started to bend it about. 'No doubt Ivor will be delighted to see you. I expect he's rung you a few times since you left?'

'No, not once.' Ellis looked surprised. 'I've rung him, though.' She clasped her hands and studied them. 'He usually prefers me to take the initiative. He's a bit'—she hesitated, took a breath and finished—'a bit shy.'

He sat, swinging his leg, saying nothing. The paper clip was opened out into a straight line now. 'Will you do something for me, Cleone? Will you call on my grandmother? She'll be glad to see you. I told you she loves having young people near her.'

'Of course I will.'

'Thanks,' he said, and looked hopelessly at the mess he had made of the paper clip. It was useless now as a method of fastening things together, so he threw it away. He stood beside her, his hand resting on her shoulder, and looked at the papers in front of her.

Cleone, tense now, lowered her arms to cover the editorial and in doing so moved the protective sheet of paper. The first few lines of the editorial slipped out of hiding and caught his eye.

'What's this all about?' He read the words aloud. '"Let's face it, the fashion business is about making money."' He glanced at her, saw with interest her flaming cheeks and reached out to pick up the sheet of paper.

She clutched at his hand with frightened fingers. 'It's just—just something I've written. It's not finished, not fit to be read by anyone yet.'

He said quietly, 'If you will give me back the use of my hand, Miss Aston...' She released it at once. 'Right. Now I should be glad if you would let me read what you have written.'

When he spoke in those authoritative tones, she could not refuse. She handed it to him and waited uneasily for his reaction.

'Let's face it,' she had written, 'the fashion business is about making money. And the money these days is in young people's pockets. They have no ties, no expenses, no responsibilities except those they create for themselves. They can spend their money where they like.

'And they like clothes—a lot of clothes, a variety of clothes. They like the boutiques because they provide the clothes they want. They like to pick and choose, so they go from one boutique to another doing just that.

'Like selecting ingredients for an *hors d'œuvre*, they

shop around, buying here a skirt, there a sleeveless top; a pair of slacks here, and boots or belts and bags there. Being young, they have an inborn feeling for colour, an unerring knowledge of the fashion of the day. They know just what they want and go all out to get it.

'*Couture?* Most of them have never heard of it. Patterns adapted from the great designers? They wouldn't give a "thank you" for that. They have their own designers, young ones mostly, who give them the clothes they want to wear—throw-away clothes that don't hang on in the wardrobe from one season to the next because of what they cost to buy; practical clothes, easy to wear and non-restricting, that can be put on—and taken off—as the fancy takes them.

'*Couture* for the older generation? It's beyond their pockets. It's just a beautiful dream, a fabulous out-of-reach photograph in a "glossy" magazine.

'That leaves *couture* right out in the cold. And there it will stay until one day it fades away. *Couture* was a dream —and a woman these days won't pay for dreams—they're too expensive. So she goes for what she can afford—the real thing, within reach, there in her hand.'

He read it through to the end. He said, with deliberate calm, 'You aren't going to use this, of course.'

She bristled defensively. 'I don't see why not.'

He threw it down. 'It's out of the question. Quite unsuitable. Surely you realise that?'

'It may be unsuitable for the publication as it stands, but I've angled it for the future, taking into account the changes that are coming in the style of the magazine.'

'You're taking too much for granted, Cleone.' Still that iron control of his temper, but the warning note came through. 'I will not be pressurised into taking any action which I am not entirely convinced is right. Don't think I'm not aware of the "wearing-away" tactics you're adopting where I'm concerned.'

She drooped, facing defeat. 'I still don't see what's

wrong with conditioning readers to change. That way it's so gradual they won't even notice . . .'

'Look here, young woman.' He seized her chin with fingers of steel and jerked her face up to his.

'One day, not so far distant, you and I are going to have a showdown. You've said things to me that I wouldn't have tolerated from any other employee in this firm. So far, and God knows why, I've let you get away with it. But I'm warning you, if you flout my instructions and use that editorial, you—will—be—dismissed.' His eyes, ruthless and hard, held hers. 'This is not the first time I've threatened you with dismissal, but by heaven, I mean it now! Do you understand?'

'Yes,' she whispered.

'Right. Tear that editorial up and we'll have no more trouble.' His expression softened and he kissed her upturned lips. 'Goodbye, Cleone. Have a good weekend.' He smiled and left her.

When she had recovered her breath, she picked up the editorial and, with a sigh, pushed it into a drawer.

She felt like a stranger walking into her own home. Her mother hugged her and her father kissed her on the cheek. Even her bedroom looked different. It was shabbier than she remembered. Her personal possessions might have belonged to another girl, they were so meaningless now. Yet it was not so long ago that this room had been the centre of her whole world.

She phoned Ivor after tea and had to accustom herself all over again to his lukewarm responses.

'Shall we meet?' he asked.

Good heavens, she thought, of course we'll meet! Why didn't he say, 'We *must* meet, tonight—now. I'm coming round at once.'

They arranged a time for him to call for her the following afternoon.

Next morning she took a bus to Ellis's grandmother's

cottage. She was welcomed by two arms, stretched towards her, and pulled gently down to kiss a wrinkled, peach-soft cheek.

'My dear child,' Mrs. Firse said, her voice uneven with emotion, 'how lovely to see you. Sit down here,' she pulled the footstool forward, 'and tell me all about yourself. How's my grandson? And do you see much of him? And are you enjoying your work?'

Cleone answered the questions one by one. 'I've seen quite a lot of him. I've been out with him once or twice—on business engagements, of course,' she hastened to add.

'And have you seen his flat?'

'Yes. Ellis—I mean Mr. Firse'—the old lady did not seem to notice her slip—'took me there one evening after we had been out together.'

'Isn't it beautiful, my dear? The furniture, the curtains . . .'

'Yes, it's beautiful,' she answered, her voice flat.

'What about my son? Have you met him yet?'

'Yes, I've met him twice.' She glanced quickly at the old lady. 'He's not an easy person to get to know, is he?' Mrs. Firse shook her head. 'But the second time I went to his house, I tried on a dress for him. He talked to me then——'

'My dear, if my son talked to you, then you're honoured indeed. He does not usually notice anyone outside his sphere, let alone talk to them.' With a nod of her head, she indicated a drawer across the room. 'If you would be kind enough to open that and take out something wrapped in tissue . . .'

Cleone found the packet and handed it to her.

'You remember, Cleone, I promised you some lace? Well, here it is.' She lifted up three pieces of exquisite crochet. 'I wondered if you could use them as sleeves—see, they are shaped to fit an armhole. And this could be a collar, or used as an insertion in a blouse or dress.'

'Mrs. Firse, it's wonderful!' Cleone kissed her cheek again, sweet-smelling and smooth. 'How can I thank you?'

'No need for thanks, my dear. I enjoyed doing it. Now put it away and don't forget it when you go.'

Cleone made some tea and they drank it and talked again. As she was leaving, Mrs. Firse said to her, 'Would you give my grandson a message, my child? Tell him I send my love and that I'm still waiting, and would he please hurry, because the days are going by. He will know what I mean.'

Cleone laughed, knowing that the old lady was referring to that great-grandchild she was longing for. She thought, with some sadness, it was unlikely that her hopes would be fulfilled in that respect for a very long time indeed.

Cleone walked back the way she knew so well, over the fields and through the woods, trying in vain to recapture the old feeling of freedom and contentment. She even lay down under the same tree, her tree, staring up at the sky through the branches and the full green leaves. But she shut her eyes in the end, because all she could see, wherever she looked, was the face of Ellis Firse, not smiling, but hard and angry as he had looked after reading the editorial.

He was her life now, and she could not escape from the knowledge. He was all she wanted and he was as out of reach as the sun in the sky.

She called into the newspaper office, wanting suddenly to see old friends. But even they seemed different. Mike was there and one or two of the reporters. Mr. Riley shook her heartily by the hand and questioned her closely about her work. He wished her luck and foresaw great things for her.

Mike looked her over and said with the quick perspicacity of youth, 'That's not the real Cleone, not the one we knew. You've changed. The real Cleone used to come in from her calls with leaves sticking to her from lying under the trees and staring at the sky.' He looked at her feet. 'I bet they're a darned sight cleaner these days. No walking about barefoot to make them dirty!'

She felt an overwhelming desire to cry and at that

moment would have given it all up for the happiness and peace of mind she used to know.

She spent the afternoon with Ivor. He said he had missed her, but his kiss was as restrained as ever. As she tried to respond to him, she thought of that other kiss which had aroused her beyond belief.

They met again next day and discussed their savings and the house they would buy one day soon. Cleone did most of the talking, telling him about her work and her experiences. In the end it became such a strain that it was almost with relief that she parted from him at her door.

First thing Monday morning she dialled Ellis's extension on her internal telephone. She had to give him his grandmother's message.

His secretary answered. 'Hallo, Carol,' Cleone said, 'is Mr. Firse available?'

'I'm sorry, Miss Aston, but he's not here. He's gone abroad.'

Dazed, Cleone echoed, 'Gone abroad?'

'Yes, didn't he tell you? He's gone to the United States.'

'How—how long will he be away?'

'Three weeks to a month. He wasn't sure when he would be back. Was it important? I've got his hotel address. He'll be there a couple of weeks. After that, he's staying at a private house—having a short holiday, I believe, before returning home.'

'No,' said Cleone, 'it's not important. Thanks for telling me.'

She rang off. 'So he's gone away,' she thought, 'about a month. Thirty-one days before I see him again. He said, on Friday, "Goodbye, Cleone." But why didn't he tell me? Why should he tell me? I'm just an employee, as he keeps saying. But he kissed me. What does a kiss mean to a man like that? He kisses all his women.'

Sarah came in. Cleone said, as though she were sleepwalking, 'Mr. Firse has gone abroad, to America. He'll be away about a month.'

'Has he?' said Sarah, only half interested. 'He'll be seeing his lady-love over there. Some rich girl-friend. She's the daughter of the owner of an enormous department store. She's also a fashion buyer for the firm and comes over regularly to see the François collections.'

'So she'll be coming soon to see the latest one?'

'Probably. I expect he'll bring her back with him. Do they lay it on when she comes! She's treated like a queen. After all, think of the money she brings with her in the form of orders for François creations.'

'What's her name?'

'Something like Connar. That's it, Karin Connar.'

'Is she nice-looking?'

'That's an understatement. She's breathtaking. Puts Annabelle and Maria and Co. in the shade.'

When Sarah had gone, Cleone wandered to the window. She saw the view and her eyes hunted for green. She must see some greenery again, walk on grass, smell the flowers, listen to birdsong. She thought of the park she had passed on the bus. 'I'll buy some sandwiches,' she promised herself, 'and take them there for lunch.'

She sat on a bench and ate the sandwiches and fed the ducks on the lake, pretending she couldn't hear the traffic noise, or smell the air which was polluted with exhaust fumes.

After that, whenever the weather was fine, she lunched in the park.

One morning she was transferring a packet of sandwiches —she had made them up that morning at home—from her drawer into her bag when Rick wandered in.

'Where are you going?' he asked, watching her. She told him.

'If I joined you, would you object to my company?'

'Of course not,' she said, and they went together to the park.

They made a habit of it after that and when it rained

they went across to a local sandwich bar. Rick was good company and his humour helped the days to pass more quickly than she had hoped.

Ellis overstayed his time in America. Four weeks passed and still he did not return. Cleone wondered miserably if he was busy getting engaged or even married to his fabulous girl-friend.

Sometimes in the evenings, Rick took her to a film, or they would dance somewhere. They never spent much money. After a while, he started kissing her. She didn't mind. It meant nothing to her and she hoped it was the same with him.

Occasionally she phoned Ivor, but the conversation between them was so slow and so forced on her part that she gave up phoning and decided to write to him instead.

One evening she took Rick to a fashion show and he made a few sketches. It was orthodox and uninspiring and afterwards, to cheer themselves up, they went dancing. Rick took her home and she invited him in for coffee.

He kissed her, and as his kisses became more demanding, she knew her invitation had been a mistake. She fended him off successfully and told him she was tired and would he please go home.

Reluctantly he left and she flopped hopelessly into bed. She was numb with longing for Ellis Firse and had even stopped counting the days. She began to think that he would never come back.

She went to work next day heavy-eyed and listless. She stared out of the window, seeing nothing but a blur of buildings, and wishing she had never taken the job. She wished she could pack up and go home and return to being the girl she used to be.

The door opened, but she did not turn.

'Cleone?'

She swung round, her heartbeats nearly choking her.

'Ellis!' How she stopped herself from running into his

arms she never knew. But she could not wipe the welcome from her eyes or the smile from her parted lips.

Then she remembered. Karin Connar would be with him. She became composed and with studied calm said, 'Welcome back, Mr. Firse.'

'Don't mention it, Miss Aston.' The words were sarcastic, but they were spoken with a smile. He looked at her closely. 'You look tired. Been living it up in my absence?'

She sat down. 'Not really. A few outings with Rick. We went to a dance last night.'

His eyes narrowed. 'Did you now?' He came closer. 'Late nights don't suit a country kitten, Miss Aston.' He draped himself on the edge of her desk and the urge to stretch out her hand and touch him was overpowering.

'Did you come back alone?'

'Yes. Shouldn't I have done?'

'I thought—I was told you might have company.' She watched him. 'Someone called Karin?'

He looked down and grew vague. 'No, she's still there. She wanted me to delay my return still further and fly here with me, but I had urgent business to attend to. She's coming in a week or so to see my father's collection.' He looked up. 'Talking of my father, he wants to see you. Something about another fitting. Would you mind?'

'Mind?' she thought. 'I'd do anything to please you or your father—anything to get just a little nearer to you.'

'Not at all,' she said aloud.

'This evening?'

'If you like. I can get on with the dress I'm making afterwards, I suppose.'

'So if I picked you up about seven?' She nodded. 'Good.' He stood up but seemed reluctant to leave. Then she remembered his grandmother's message. When she gave it to him, he laughed and walked to the window.

'So she's still waiting, is she? Never mind, she may not have to wait much longer.'

She wondered what his cryptic statement meant and decided miserably that it would not be long before he announced his engagement to his American heiress.

He turned at the door. 'Where are you lunching?'

'I bring sandwiches now.'

He laughed. 'Copying me?'

'Not really. When it's fine, I go to the park and eat them there.'

'Alone?'

'Not always. Sometimes Rick joins me.'

'Oh. Quite a friendship blossoming between you.' The sarcasm was there again, but this time he was not smiling.

She looked out at the sunshine. 'I'm going alone today. Rick can't come.'

Then he looked out at the sunshine. 'The weather tempts me. Would you object to my company in place of the art editor's?'

'*You* come with me?'

'Why not? I could do with a few breaths of polluted fresh air—British variety. It's a fraction less piquant than the stuff they manufacture in the States. And I'm in holiday mood.'

'Well,' she looked doubtful, 'all right. Do you want to share my sandwiches?'

'I'll bring my own, thanks. Give me a ring when you're going.' He went out.

At lunch-time he insisted that they took a taxi. 'I've nothing against buses,' he said, 'except the jams they get themselves into.'

'And taxis don't?'

He shrugged. 'At least it's more comfortable being jammed up in a taxi.'

They were delivered to the park gates and wandered round until they found an empty bench. Ellis seemed content to sit beside her, watching the passers-by or commenting on the good taste of sandwiches after more than five weeks without them.

Now and then Cleone would look at his profile, telling

herself that it was not a dream and that he was really there at her side. He shared her cakes—she had made them herself, she said, and he made appreciative noises—and her flask of coffee.

'I've only the top of the flask to drink from,' she told him, 'no other cup.'

'I don't mind. I'll drink from the other side.' He grinned and she marvelled at his carefree mood. So the cup passed between them and she noticed that he didn't turn it round. 'Tastes better this way,' he said, as he took a sip.

When they had finished he asked, 'Where are you going after this—back to the office?'

'No. To a fashion show.' She named a famous store in central London.

'Right. We'll take a taxi.'

'We'? So he was going with her. She spent the time getting there trying to work out why. It couldn't be that he liked her company. She decided that it must be that 'holiday mood' he said he was suffering from.

They sat together on the chairs that had been placed along the sides of the raised catwalk. While Cleone studied the programme, Ellis looked slightly bored and flicked through his diary. The background music became sweet and soothing and this seemed to be the signal for the fashion show to begin.

With subtlety and skill, tall, slender young women showed the clothes stocked by the store. There were capes and suits, some trimmed with fur, others faultlessly tailored. There were chiffon dresses and evening gowns. There was knitwear teamed with skirts or trousers, separates and ski clothes.

One of the models moved with light, quick steps to the end of the catwalk, paused in front of Ellis and smiled down at him. He smiled back.

'Another of his women?' Cleone wondered, and could not stop herself whispering, 'She seemed to know you.'

He whispered back, 'She does. Her name, if you must

know, is Valentina. She used to work for my father.'

'She's attractive,' Cleone heard herself say.

'She certainly is.' He grinned. 'Very decorative at a dinner table.'

'Better than Karin?' she asked, getting annoyed with herself for persisting.

'Definitely not,' he answered. 'Karin is quite exceptional.' His grin held malice as he watched the sudden despairing movement of her hands.

At the end of the show, Cleone risked his annoyance and ventured, 'This is where your father should be—at the quality end of the ready-to-wear market. Look at the famous names on this programme. The prices are high compared with the lower end of ready-to-wear, but certainly not beyond the pockets of women of reasonable means. Your father's clothes are so exclusive, their appeal can only be to the really rich.'

'I'm aware of that, Miss Aston.' His tone was sharp. 'You've made your point *ad nauseam*, if I may say so.'

'I'm sorry,' she said with a sigh.

They wandered round the women's department and Cleone exclaimed with delight at the clothes on display, admiring their cut and the cloth from which they were made.

'Do you call this work?' asked Ellis.

'Of course it is. This is how I get to know the trends and the kind of clothes the shops are selling. I also get my ideas for the magazine this way—not that I'm allowed to use them there.' She looked at him reproachfully.

'Yes, well, we'll steer off that subject. Let's appear to be friends, at least in public.'

She tutted impatiently—she could get nowhere with him. She felt like a moth trying desperately to find a way into a lighted room through a pane of glass.

A red velvet dress caught her eye. She found a mirror and held the dress against her.

'Are you contemplating buying it?' Ellis asked. She

didn't seem to hear, being apparently carried away on a dream. He looked at the price tag. 'A little beyond your means, isn't it?'

'Of course. But that doesn't stop me looking at them. Sometimes I try them on,' she added wistfully, replacing the dress with a sigh.

They walked on to the next department. 'Where does your father get his ideas from?' she asked. 'Does he visit art galleries and study the paintings, as some designers do?'

'I've never asked him. I told you, somehow we can't communicate.'

She remembered his cool, off-hand attitude the evening she went to his father's house for the first fitting. 'Have you ever really tried?'

'My relationship with my father is my own concern.'

She refused to be squashed, saying brightly, 'I don't get on with my father, but I get on with yours. It's odd, isn't it?' She looked at him consideringly. 'Perhaps you'd get on better with mine.'

She saw his curious smile and realised too late the implication of her words.

'Is that a subtle way of saying, "Come and meet my parents"?'

She coloured deeply and replied with spirit, disregarding in the heat of the moment his position in the firm, 'No, it wasn't. I would never try to pin you down to anything. I've watched you in action, with your girl-friends. You're as elusive as—as a dandelion seed flying about in the wind.'

He merely smiled and let it go. They reached the shoe department.

'Ah yes, shoes,' he remarked, staring pointedly at her feet. 'A bone of contention between us. Looking at them displayed around us jogs my memory.'

She did not take him up on his provocative statement, and wandered round, doing a quick financial calculation in her head.

'Would you mind,' she asked, 'if I tried some on? I need

a new pair and these styles look so good——'

'Go ahead, Cinderella. I'm in no hurry. I told my secretary to keep this afternoon free of appointments since it's my first day back.'

Twenty minutes later, he was sitting forward, patiently watching her trying to make a final choice between two pairs of shoes.

'What's wrong with those black ones?' he asked, pointing.

'Nothing at all,' she answered, looking at them longingly, 'except the price. I couldn't possibly afford to pay that just for one pair of shoes.'

She looked at the pair on her feet and sighed. 'These are a lot cheaper. It'll have to be these.' Still she seemed to hesitate and her eyes drifted to the others.

The assistant, eager to make the best sale possible, said to Ellis, 'Don't you think your wife's feet looked lovely in those, sir? They're a lovely quality, sir.'

Ellis straightened in his seat and grinned. 'You know, darling, she's right. You should have that pair.'

Cleone gave him a murderous look. 'You know I can't afford it,' she hissed, 'and anyway, I'm not your . . .'

'Right,' said Ellis to the saleswoman, 'we'll take that black pair, please, and while we're about it,' his look dared Cleone to interrupt the transaction, 'we'll have the other pair, too.'

He produced his wallet and took out some notes. 'Does that cover it?'

'Oh yes, sir,' she gushed, delight making her bob a curtsy like a Victorian servant, 'I'm sure your wife will be most satisfied, sir.' She bustled away.

'How could you?' Cleone reproached him, slipping her feet into her own shoes. 'Now I'll have to pay you back and——'

'They're a gift, Cleone. It also brought your infuriating dither to a speedy end. And,' he held up his hand to silence her protests, 'a fashion editor working for Firse Publications should always be as well dressed as possible.'

She flared, 'So I don't dress to your liking?'

'I didn't say that. Now be quiet. The assistant's coming back and if you're not careful, she'll notice the absence of a wedding ring and I'll have to buy you one if only to make an honest woman of you!'

That did silence her. She pulled on her left-hand glove and walked on while Ellis took the parcel and pocketed the change.

In the taxi on the way back he said dryly, 'I'm overwhelmed by your gratitude.'

'I'm sorry, Ellis. Thank you very much for buying me those shoes.' Her look was defiant. 'I've decided how to repay you for them—by working late until I've settled the debt.'

'Don't be an idiot. I don't want payment from you.'

'All the same, I will.'

He stretched out his arm and ruffled her hair.

'Seven this evening,' he reminded her as he gave her the shoes. They parted outside his door.

CHAPTER VII

THE tight-fitting black velvet trousers and matching waistcoat which Cleone wore over a long-sleeved sweater made Ellis's eyebrows rise. 'Another Aston creation? Made by Cleone's own fair hands?'

'Of course. Do you like it?'

' "Like" is hardly adequate. The outfit is stunning, the general effect devastating. What are you trying to do—seduce *me*, instead of the other way round?'

'No,' she laughed, 'just trying to look nice.'

'Nice? *Nice?* That word, in my vocabulary, when placed in front of "*girl*" implies that she is slightly prim and rather ineffective. In those clothes, you're——' He stopped, took a breath with difficulty. 'Come on, let's go before I begin to show you just how effective you are.'

François' eyebrows flickered perceptibly when Cleone entered the fitting room, but he made no comment. The atmosphere was one of hustle and rush, rising almost to hysteria in the workrooms which adjoined the fitting room. The excited voices of the girls and women working there came through the locked door, making conversation difficult.

Ellis went out—Cleone supposed he had gone to find Annabelle—and the dress was carried in. The fitting was satisfactory, the gown perfect. Antoine came in while Cleone was wearing it and whistled appreciatively.

'You'll be a model yet,' he commented, inspecting her with a professional eye. For his benefit she rotated and posed as if she were displaying a dress at a fashion show and he applauded. 'You've got what it takes. Style, panache, elegance, the—er—physique, the lot. All you need to do is to grow a bit, and you're in.'

She swept him a deep curtsy.

'Another admirer, Miss Aston?' Ellis said behind her, his eyes glinting. 'You collect them like some women collect hats.'

'It's a pity your father hasn't got a vacancy for a model, Mr. Firse,' Antoine said jokingly.

'You think she's got what it takes, do you? Well, Miss Aston, now you know—when I fire you from your job, my father will accept you into his *ménage* with open arms.'

François came in, laughing at his son's remark. He inspected the evening gown in detail and said he was quite satisfied.

'Is it ready for your client now?' Cleone asked as the dress was taken away.

'It is,' he told her. 'I must thank you sincerely for your co-operation.'

'Where's Mother?' Ellis asked his father, as Cleone combed the tangles out of her hair.

'Staying with the Everetts. You know how she hates the run-up to collections.'

Annabelle came in, shadowed by Maria. They both exclaimed, 'Ellis darling, how I've missed you!' in affected tones and took an arm each, peering up into his face and willing him to favour them with a kiss.

Gently but firmly he extricated himself from their clutches and sauntered across to Cleone. He put his arm across her shoulders and she laughed openly at his evasive manoeuvre. He smiled down at her and she played up to him, moving closer to his side, watching the eyes of the two girls grow wide with astonishment, then narrow with annoyance. They eventually walked out in disgust.

Cleone twisted away as soon as they had gone.

'Tricky, that,' she said with a gleam in her eye. 'At least I keep my so-called admirers apart. They're easier to handle that way.'

He advanced on her. 'Are they indeed?'

The door opened and a girl walked across to Cleone, holding in her arms a large dress box. 'For you, Miss Aston, with the compliments of the House of François.'

The designer himself stood in the doorway and watched.

Cleone was stunned, took the box in her outstretched arms and stared down at it.

'It's the dress, Miss Aston,' François said.

'But—but why? I thought it was for your client.'

'It was. She changed her mind and decided not to have it. I am therefore making a present of it to you. A gift from an established designer to one who is just beginning.'

'But I—I can't take it . . .'

'It's a gift, Miss Aston. It's no use to me now. No other client of mine has those measurements, nor would it suit their tastes.'

She looked at Ellis for reassurance and he nodded.

Still breathless, she said to François, 'Saying thank you seems so inadequate——'

He held up his hand. 'Say no more. I'm glad you like it,

and I hope you will wear it for the ball which will be held after the showing of my collection. You will be invited to it, together with other selected members of the press. Now I must go. I have a great deal of work to do.'

She thanked him again and he left them.

'I'll take you home, Cleone,' Ellis said.

She was still dazed when he carried the box into her flat.

'It's fabulous, Ellis. It must be worth hundreds of pounds!'

'It is. It's *couture*.' He whispered in her ear, 'The real thing!'

'Thank you for bringing me home,' she said, and waited for him to leave, but he didn't move.

'Can I take you out for a meal?'

'Thanks, but I think I'll have something light at home. I want to get on with cutting out my dress.'

'Oh.' He seemed deflated and looked about him. 'What do you mean by "something light"?'

'I've got a cheese and egg flan in the fridge which I made yesterday . . .'

'That sounds delicious. You—er—couldn't spare a piece for me, could you?'

'Of course I could.' She tried to keep the pleasure from her eyes. She put out her best place mats and found a candle to light and set the table for two. She heated the flan and made a trifle, topping it with whipped cream, and as they were eating the meal, Ellis commented with appreciation on her culinary skill.

'I hope Ivor appreciates what a bargain he's getting. When he's got you, what man could ask for more?'

She knew by the lift of his eyebrow that he was not being sincere. He looked round.

'Soft lights, but no sweet music, Cleone? No record player?'

'Can't afford one. I'm saving up, remember.'

'Oh yes. For that house you're going to share with Ivor.'

There was amusement in his voice.

It irritated her so much she said, 'Yes, it shouldn't be long now.'

'Seen much of your fiancé?' The tone was deliberately casual.

'Not since that weekend I went home.'

'You *must* be in love!'

His cynicism goaded her still more, but her biting reply was cut off by the ring of the telephone.

Cleone answered. 'Who's that? Oh, Rick.'

There was a short sardonic laugh from the table.

'No, I'm busy, Rick. I'm making a dress. No, I'm sorry.' She turned her back on her guest who, by now, was laughing softly. 'I'd rather not have company while I'm working, Rick.' There came a loud baiting laugh from behind her. 'No, you can't come. Not tonight.' She rang off, her face pink.

Ellis draped an arm over the back of his chair and grinned. 'So you keep your admirers apart, do you? They're easier to handle that way, I believe you said.'

He got up and walked towards her. He was kissing her before she knew he had started. The pink in her cheeks had become scarlet by the time she managed to twist out of his arms.

They washed up together and she commented on how domesticated he was for a well-to-do bachelor.

He remarked casually, 'When one's contemplating marriage, it's a good thing to cultivate the domestic arts.'

It was a statement that sobered her up as effectively as a cold shower. Now she had had it from his own mouth that he intended marrying Karin Connar, the girl he had gone to America to see. But she doubted whether any husband of hers would ever have to worry about doing the washing up.

While she spread her material on the floor and cut it out, Ellis sat in an armchair, legs stretched in front of him, and read the newspaper.

'This is what it would be like to be married to him.' The thought sprang from the shadows of her mind and she had to argue with it fiercely before it would consent to go back into hiding again.

It was some time before her peace of mind was restored, but she managed in the end to calm herself by concentrating on the work in front of her.

As she knelt on the floor snipping at the material, she said thoughtfully, 'It's so silly to keep on doing things by hand.'

Ellis lowered the paper. 'What do you mean by that?'

'It's so out of date.'

'I suppose you're back on the same old subject. I suppose you mean my father.'

'Well,' she mused, deaf to the sharpness in his voice, 'so many things in the fashion trade are done by machinery now that were once traditionally done by hand. Automation is taking over.'

'Is it really?'

She disregarded his sarcasm and went on, immersed in her own thoughts, 'Did you know that man-made fibres can be bonded—that is, glued—together, making stitching unnecessary? One day there will probably be garments on sale that contain no stitches at all! There are machines that can hem both sides of a piece of material at once and sew on buttons.'

She looked up at him. 'Doesn't your father know this? Doesn't he realise that if he doesn't change his ideas soon, he'll be left behind? Can't you persuade him to break into the ready-to-wear market like the other *couturiers* and open a boutique somewhere?'

'Here we go again,' Ellis sighed, folding up the newspaper. 'After an interval of five weeks, I scent the signs of pressure. I suppose you think you've fed me into a good mood and I'll be amenable . . .' Then he threw himself back in the armchair and shouted with laughter.

'What's the matter?'

'I've just been struck by the irony of the situation. There you are, crouched on the floor over your precious material, cutting it out—by hand—with the utmost precision. Then you'll proceed to fit it—by hand, sew it—by hand and no doubt finish it off with trimming and so on—by hand. And you've got the cheek to preach to me about machinery and automation and mass-production, and urge me to persuade my father to abandon his old-fashioned methods!'

'*I* haven't gone into business,' she pointed out, feeling that he had got the better of her. 'The circumstances can't be compared.'

He watched her for a while. 'You know, if you analyse that sales talk you've just given me, it reveals that you're getting farther and farther away from your ideal—the real thing.' She shook her head violently. 'Oh, but you are, Cleone. You may deny it, but as an impartial observer, I can see it.' He leaned forward, caught her chin and looked into her face. 'You've changed, you know.'

'Mike said that when I went home that weekend. But I haven't changed fundamentally. I know I haven't.'

'Oh, but you have.' He released her and leaned back again, stretching out his legs and resting his head on his hands. 'You've grown up. You'd no more throw a shoe at anyone nowadays than you would a grand piano.' His voice seemed to hold a touch of regret. He reached into his pocket for a cigarette. 'And I'm willing to predict that you'll change even more.' He flicked his lighter. 'Like all the rest of them, you'll lose your innocence, your wide-eyed approach to life. You'll become cynical, blasé, man-eating. You've started already.' He nodded his head towards the telephone. 'That call tonight. Poor Ivor won't get a look in.' He drew on his cigarette and leaned back. 'He'll be left at the gate squatting on his haunches, ears flopping, dejected and rejected, while you inside . . .' His eyes said the rest.

'And who,' she asked defensively, 'will be the one to start me on my feminine "Rake's Progress"? Who'll be on the inside while Ivor waits outside?'

He smoked in silence for a few minutes, regarding her thoughtfully. 'Now that,' he said softly, 'is a good question, a very good question.'

Her heart began to pound at the look in his eyes and the meaning in his voice. She bent over her work again, trying to puzzle out how the atmosphere between them had changed so subtly. Last night she had had a tussle with Rick to get him off the premises. Tonight? she wondered, and did not know the answer.

After that the silence was profound and tormenting. Now and then Cleone would look up and find Ellis's eyes upon her. Confused, she would concentrate even harder on the dress, tacking it here and making tucks and darts there.

Abruptly she said, 'I feel like some coffee. Will you have some?'

He nodded and followed her into the kitchen. It was dark now and he stood at the uncurtained window gazing at the lights in the buildings opposite.

At last he said, 'Are you happy, Cleone?'

'You mean in my work? Yes, I'm happy.'

'You say it without enthusiasm.' He turned and watched her arranging the cups on the tray. 'I suppose you're missing the green fields around your home. Your personality being what it is you probably can't accept the brick and concrete jungle of the city.'

She didn't answer immediately. She could not tell him that wherever she went now was a wilderness if he was not there, that she could even tolerate the 'brick and concrete jungle' if he shared it with her.

She shrugged and said, smiling, 'You're just my employer, aren't you? Why should you be worrying about whether I'm happy or not? If I liked, if I couldn't stand the job at any price, I could just give notice and leave, couldn't I?'

'M'm.' He faced her, his expression cynical. 'There's

always Ivor to run to, isn't there?'

She let that go. It was late and she was tired, overtired from her late night with Rick and from the strain it had become entertaining Ellis Firse.

They drank their coffee and she hoped he would go, but he made no move to leave. She took the pieces of material she had tacked together and held them against herself in front of the bedroom mirror. Her eyes moved sharply and she saw his reflection as he stood in the doorway behind her. Something in his face made her swing round, frightened.

'Cleone?' he said, and there was a question in his voice. She could hardly bear the throb of her heart as he approached. He took away the dress and threw it on a chair. Then he pulled her to him convulsively like a man who had waited for something for an interminable length of time and had now reached the end of his endurance.

His mouth explored her throat and face and found her lips at last. In his arms she felt an overpowering release from tension, as if this was what her body had been waiting for all the weeks he had been away, all the days she had longed for his return and all the hours without his voice or touch.

The straying, caressing urgency of his hands was almost more than she could bear.

'Let me love you, Cleone,' he whispered, 'let me stay. For God's sake, let me love you.'

'This is madness,' a small voice cried, and she had to listen. She felt his need of her sucking in her willpower, but she had to listen to that voice. In her thoughts she threw up her hands—she would not drown. She would not submit to his need, his urgent, passing need of her. Had she been any one of his women, he would have used the same words, made the same plea. He did not love her any more than he loved them.

She clutched at driftwood, pushing aside her love and her longing for his love.

'Ivor,' she cried like a man shrieking for help inside a burning building, 'I'm going to marry Ivor!' And she said Ivor's name over and over again until Ellis tore himself away from her and walked out into the darkness.

She did not know how she lived through the days that followed. She had not seen Ellis since the night he had left her. Time and again she felt an overpowering urge to dial his extension just to hear his voice.

Her friendship with Rick continued and she managed to keep him under control by telling him she was engaged to be married. He probably knew, she thought, that if he persisted in his demands he would lose her altogether.

She had phoned Ivor and invited him to stay in town one weekend. She thought that if she could produce her fiancé in person, it might help to stave off Rick's amorous advances.

The formal invitation to the ball which was to be held after the showing of the François collection had arrived. She was permitted to take a guest and she asked Rick if he would like to partner her. He said he was delighted to be given the chance of moving in such exalted circles.

She kept to her resolve to work off her debt to Ellis for the shoes he had bought her. In fact she was more than ever determined to do so. She had stayed late three times already.

One evening she worked on, having warned the caretaker in advance, and delayed her tea until she had made considerable headway with the paperwork which seemed to have piled up.

It was the day Ellis had passed her on the stairs as if he had not known her. Now she felt a headache coming on. She pushed aside her work and rested her head on her hands. She was depressed and tired. She wished she could understand Ellis's attitude towards her. She wished he would tell her what wrong she had done him. Apart from hurting his pride, she could think of nothing else.

Everyone had gone. The silence was like a blanket and she burrowed into it and slept. She awoke with a painful neck, aching arm muscles and a gnawing hunger inside her. When she saw the time she panicked. Nearly ten o'clock, and she had told the caretaker she would be leaving at nine.

She put away the papers, pulled on her coat, grabbed her handbag and ran to the lift. It took her swiftly to the ground floor. She groped for the light switches and turned them on. She pushed against the entrance doors. They were locked. The rear entrance—that would still be open. Of course the caretaker had not locked her in. But the rear doors were bolted and barred.

She forced herself to keep calm, walking along the corridor and trying all the doors. They were locked. Then she saw the lurking shadows. They were everywhere, on the walls, the ceilings, the stairs. She drew a gasping breath as she saw her own shadow towering over her, caught by a trick of the light and flung, enormous and menacing, up the walls of the staircase.

Through the glass partitions there were black shapes—filing cabinets, tables, chairs, all losing their everyday solidity and becoming wispy phantoms in the half-light.

She made for the lift and the door clanged to, shutting her in. She was lifted an interminable distance upwards—would it ever stop? At the ninth floor the lift doors opened and their soulless mechanical obedience assumed a menace of their own. Even in the sanctuary of her room she could hear the unearthly stillness, but there was nothing soft and sleep-inducing about it now. Now the tentacles of silence reached out to get her.

Ellis, she thought, he'll come. What was his number? She searched for the directory, pawed through the pages. There it was—Firse, E. F. She dialled and waited, a smile on her face. Now it wouldn't be long.

There was no reply. She held on . . . and on . . . and on. She knew it was hopeless, but the intermittent sound echoing in that empty flat was in itself a comfort, a contact with the outside world. She gave up at last and put the receiver down. Then there was nothing to hear but the silence. Now it was suffocating her. She walked about her room just to hear her own footsteps. She stared out at the darkness, saw below the moving lights of the traffic, realised with a stab of terror how far away the ninth floor was from the ground.

She turned away, fighting claustrophobia, feeling the walls coming in at her. The phone—she would try again. She dialled, her heart hammering, heard the ring at the other end remain unanswered.

Half past eleven and hunger was clawing at her like a raging animal. The silence was a great crouching creature waiting to spring. She thought she heard a noise on the stairs and stifled a scream. Now she was imagining things. She walked up and down like a caged tiger.

She lifted the phone again. It was midnight now. He *must* be back. But his flat was empty. Perhaps she was dialling the wrong number. She checked and rechecked and checked again.

Nearly one o'clock. He *must* be in by now! No reply. All night? she asked herself, was he staying out all night? She felt sick and slumped in her seat. Perhaps he was in and had gone to bed. Perhaps he was asleep and couldn't hear the phone. She grabbed the receiver and dialled again. Now she would not ring off until that phone was answered.

She held on and on and on. And a voice said, 'Ellis Firse here.' And she couldn't speak. She heard him asking, 'Who is it? Firse here. Hallo?'

She tried to mouth the words and he put the phone down. She screamed. She dialled again. The answer came, emphatic and irritable and just a little suspicious, 'Firse here. Who—is—that?'

'Ellis,' she whispered, 'Ellis.' That was all she could say.

'Who's that?' he repeated and she said, 'Ellis,' again.

'Will you tell me who you are?' He was angry now and no wonder, she thought.

She managed to whisper her name, then more loudly, 'Cleone Aston. I'm locked in.' Now she had communicated with him and drooped with relief.

'Locked in? Where? At your flat?'

'No, at the office. I was working late and...'

'Good grief, girl, you must be mad! Look, I'll come straight away, but it might take half an hour. Can you wait that long, or shall I tell the police?'

'No, I'll wait for you, Ellis. I'll wait for you.'

Only half an hour more of this nightmare. She dropped into her chair and half-sprawled over her desk. Ellis was coming, Ellis was on his way. She slept.

She awoke to the chiming of a distant clock and knew stark terror. She heard the clanging of the lift and she had forgotten that Ellis was coming. She stopped breathing, her eyes dilating. He rattled the door handle and called her name and she remembered. Ellis had come.

Her legs had wills of their own as she stumbled across to turn the key. He caught her as she fell. He did not seem to object to the way she clung to him, her hands gripping his shoulders, her cheek against his chest. Her breathing was shallow and fast, but she didn't cry—her relief was too deep for tears.

'When did you last eat?' he asked sharply.

'Lunch,' she whispered.

'As I thought. So I can't give you the stiff drink you obviously need. But I've got a packet of biscuits in my office...'

'I'm beyond food.'

He ignored her words and swung her into his arms. He carried her to the lift and down to the ground floor. In his office he lowered her into a chair and found the biscuits, but she turned from them.

'You're having one even if I have to force it down your throat.'

She took one and crunched it slowly, the sweetness of it pleasing to her tongue after hours of fasting. He sat on the arm of the chair and offered her another. He bit into one himself and said, 'Don't tell the others about our secret feast in the small hours. There's no knowing what conclusions they might come to!'

He put away the biscuits. 'Now I'll take you home.' He carried her to his car, wrapped her in a thick tartan rug and drove through the dark empty streets to her flat.

He insisted that she got into bed, and then he would bring her some milk. She told him not to bother.

He said firmly, 'Spoilt bachelor I may be, but I'm perfectly capable of heating milk without assistance.'

While she drank it, he sat on the bed. 'Tell me,' he said, 'why did you phone me? Why didn't you contact the police?'

She looked blank, then said, her eyes big with fatigue, 'I didn't think of anyone else. I only thought of you.'

He was silent, his face in shadow cast by her bedside lamp. He said, in an odd tone, 'Country kitten wanted me, and I didn't hear her cry for help—not until she had almost died of fright!'

'But you came.'

'Yes, I came, in the end.' He laughed shortly. 'It's almost symbolic, isn't it? The kitten became entangled in its own ball of wool. I gave you the "wool" to play with in the first place. Then I had to come and get you out of the mess.' He frowned. 'I shall never cease reproaching myself for enticing you out of your natural environment and coercing you into taking this job.'

'But you didn't really, Ellis. Don't you remember, in the end you made it so difficult for me to get it—you put up so many barriers—I thought you'd changed your mind about me.'

'My sweet innocent, I knew what I was doing. There was a method in my apparent elusiveness.'

'So you were egging me on?' She started to become indignant, but found it such a difficult emotion to sustain at so late an hour she merely tutted and shook her head.

He took out a cigarette, began to light it, changed his mind and put it away.

'Go ahead and smoke it,' Cleone said.

'No. It's not fair to pollute the air of your bedroom. After all, I'm not staying. Am I?'

He was taunting her and she turned pinker than her bed-jacket at the memory of what had happened the last time he was in her bedroom.

His smile was touched with bitterness as he said, 'I'm waiting for it.' She looked puzzled. 'For that talisman of yours, that four-letter word you utter so effectively to keep men with dishonourable intentions at bay.' He spelt it out. 'I-v-o-r.' He waited for a response but none came. 'You know,' he looked her over, 'in that pink thing you've got round your shoulders, you look big-eyed and dauntingly innocent, just as you did the first time I saw you.'

With his forefinger he traced the quilting on her bed-cover. 'If only I'd left you where you were . . .'

'I'm glad you didn't, Ellis. I like my job. I wouldn't want to leave it now.'

'Even with the limitations imposed on you from above?'

'Even with them.' She smiled. 'But those won't last for ever, will they?'

Suspicious, his head jerked up. 'Are you putting on the pressure even now, you impudent little puss, at two o'clock in the morning? Was that remark of yours a statement or a question?'

'It was a statement,' she said, with confidence.

'You're so supremely sure of getting your own way, aren't you? Do you always?'

She sighed, her eyes clouding over, her shoulders drooping. 'Not always, no.'

'Oh? And what is eluding you now?'

If she were to tell him the truth, it would be an end and a beginning.

'Sleep,' she muttered, and closed her eyes.

He got up at once and took her cup. Then he stood at the

bedside.

'I'm so sorry about all this, Ellis. Thank you for coming to get me.'

'It must have been hell.'

'It was.' She gazed up at him. 'Especially when I couldn't contact you.'

He frowned. 'I'm sorry about that. I was dining out.'

'Oh.' He saw the weary resignation in her eyes as she asked, 'And dancing?'

'No, I was dining with friends.'

'Oh,' she repeated flatly, showing that she did not believe him.

'Yes, with friends.' His tone was curt. 'With a fellow-director and his wife. Then they insisted that I went back to their place for drinks.' He stood, towering over her, his face dark with displeasure. 'I don't know what sort of image you have of me in your mind, or of the sort of life I lead, but, for the record, I'm not the pleasure-seeking womaniser you seem to think I am.'

'No?' her lips said, but her eyes told him that she didn't believe him.

'*No!*' He leaned over her intimidatingly. 'In any case, my activities in my leisure hours are not your concern!'

She blushed at the truth in his words.

'I'm sorry,' she said, turning her head aside.

He straightened and watched her thoughtfully.

'But remember,' he said, after a pause, 'the next time you're hissing and clawing at me, that I did answer your call eventually, and that I didn't let you down.'

She kept her eyes closed. What was he trying to say?

'Don't come in tomorrow, Cleone—sorry, today.'

Her eyes came open. 'But of course I must.'

He laughed. 'Don't worry, I won't fire you for that, from the job you say you like so much.'

'I'll be in,' she assured him, sliding down the bed until the bedclothes covered her chin. 'I'm not taking the risk.'

He looked nettled again. 'Exactly what sort of person do

you think I am?'

'I think you're quite capable of firing anyone, anyone at all, even me.' He shook his head, exasperated with her now. 'Goodnight, Ellis. And thanks again for rescuing me,' she whispered.

He smiled and bent down so that his face was near enough to kiss her. 'When a country kitten puts out a mayday message and I pick up her distress signals, how can I resist her cry for help?'

He straightened and she bit her lip with disappointment. 'And if there's any more nonsense about staying late——'

'It was for those shoes you bought me.'

He went on, 'If there's any more nonsense about paying for those shoes, I'll put up your salary to cover the extra time you've put in. So you can't win, can you?'

He turned out the light and closed the door behind him.

Cleone did not see Ellis again until the day of his father's fashion show. She passed him in the corridor and he was not alone. The woman hanging on his arm was tall and sparkling with carefully nurtured charm, displaying a superb figure by means of clothes that must have cost a fortune. But she had eyes that were callous and calculating, and she was the sort of woman Ellis had dismissed with contempt so often in the past.

Cleone knew that the girl must be Karin Connar. The voice was softly accented and the smile on the slightly parted lips held a special touch of intimacy as it was directed towards the man at her side.

Cleone lowered her eyes, her tired, shadowed, unhappy eyes, and passed them by.

They were together again at the fashion show. Cleone and Rick had been allotted seats near the back. She had long ago become reconciled to the fact that *Salon* was insignificant when compared with the more famous and influential fashion journals.

Karin Connar, it seemed, was being treated like a queen

and this, Cleone supposed, was inevitable. The girl had, after all, brought with her from the United States buying power to the tune of hundreds of pounds. She was also—very nearly—the managing director's fiancée. On either of these counts alone she would have merited the homage meted out to royalty.

With an experienced eye, Cleone studied Karin's clothes, then looked down at her own, at the dress she had been making the evening Ellis had walked out on her.

Although the dress fitted well—she was always meticulous about cut and fit—and although the lace which Ellis's grandmother had given her had added an exclusive touch to collar and sleeves, there was no hiding the fact that the dress was home-made. When it was set against the clothes that Karin Connar and her associates could afford to wear, it had the unmistakable stamp of 'amateur' all over it. 'House of Aston', as Ellis had jokingly referred to her efforts, and the memory brought tears to her eyes.

The atmosphere grew suffocatingly hot. Cleone pulled off her jacket and draped it across the back of her chair. The woman on her left had turned from talking to her neighbour and asked Cleone which magazine she represented.

'*Salon?* That's a Firse publication, isn't it? What are you doing at the back? Shouldn't you be in front with the élite?'

Cleone shrugged and hoped the woman's questions would stop. But the fashion writer's eagle eye alighted on the lace on Cleone's dress. She studied it for a few moments and pointed.

'François lace, isn't it? I'd recognise it anywhere.'

'Good heavens, no,' Cleone assured her, frightened by the woman's perception. 'An old lady made it, an old lady who lives near me. She spends her time doing this sort of thing.' She stopped, horrified at what she might have given away.

The journalist was plainly not convinced. 'All I can say

is, it's a mighty good copy of the lace used exclusively by François. Unobtainable anywhere, that lace, dear.' She looked into Cleone's face and asked sharply, 'Where do you live?'

'Oh,' said Cleone, vaguely, 'in the south Midlands.' That should put the woman off the scent, she thought, hastily shrugging into her jacket again. It was better to melt than to risk a repeat performance of that little interrogation.

The chatter died away as though the audience knew instinctively that the fashion show was about to begin. The music, relayed through the loudspeakers which had been placed at opposite corners of the crowded entrance hall, became persuasive and sentimental. The senior *vendeuse* took up her position on a small rostrum and announced the first two outfits.

Cleone recognised Annabelle and Maria as they decended the great sweeping staircase. The clothes they wore with such panache were *couture* at its finest and a murmur of appreciation ebbed and flowed round the audience.

As the two girls reached the foot of the staircase, one held back while the other walked from one side of the hall to the other, revealing the details of the outfit by flicks of the wrist and subtle twists of the body. Then the other followed. Each girl stopped momentarily in front of Karin and Ellis, and each girl gave Ellis a special fleeting smile.

Now and then Rick whistled softly and Cleone knew that it was appreciation for the girl inside the outfit, rather than the outfit itself. Afterwards there were drinks and a buffet and Rick put eager fingers round one glass of wine after another. When Cleone tried to restrain him, he answered, quite unabashed, that it was not often he could drink his fill without once dipping his hand into his pocket for cash.

His unending flow of jokes and drink-inspired patter became irritating, but Cleone tolerated them because they distracted her attention from Ellis and the girl he was escorting so devotedly.

When at last Rick wandered away to talk to friends,

Cleone was left alone. A hand was waved to her over the heads of the crowd and a shortish woman whom she recognised as a journalist on the staff of a well-known fashion magazine called out, 'Hallo there! Remember me?'

Cleone nodded frantically and hoped that would satisfy the woman because try as she might she could not remember her name.

A voice said, 'Drink, Miss Aston?'

Cleone managed to control the violent response which the sound of his voice aroused in her. He put a glass into her hand.

'Oh, thank you, Mr. Firse,' she said, as though they had just met.

He stood at her side and rooted about in his pocket for a cigarette. With difficulty, he got it going. He waved away the cloud of smoke and asked, without looking at her, 'You've recovered fully, I hope, from your recent ordeal? No ill effects—psychological or otherwise—as a result of being locked in?' He turned his head at last. 'I haven't seen you to ask you.'

She wanted to tell him, 'There's the phone. Couldn't you have rung me?' But all she said was, 'Yes, thank you,' and made her voice distantly polite.

There was a short tormenting silence and she rummaged about in her mind trying to unearth a subject to talk about. But Karin called to Ellis—she didn't speak because she didn't need to. They were so well attuned to each other that a smile from her dewy lips coupled with an inviting movement of her well-groomed head was sufficient to take him to her side.

'She's got him where she wants him even before they're officially engaged,' Cleone thought with disgust. She looked longingly at the door and wondered if anyone would notice if she slipped away.

The woman who had waved at her strolled across to her side.

'You're Cleone Aston, aren't you? I've just remembered

your name. In case you've forgotten, I'm Nora Whittle.'

'Of course, I remember now. Nice to see you.' Cleone managed to smile and to suppress a flick of annoyance at having had her chance of leaving snatched away.

'Warm in here,' Nora commented, fanning herself with her programme. She eyed Cleone. 'I don't know how you can stand wearing that jacket. Why don't you take it off?'

'No, it's all right.' She pulled it even tighter round her perspiring body, hoping to put the woman off the scent. She would have loved to have removed the jacket, but with the eagle eyes of so many skilled fashion writers around her, she did not dare to reveal the François lace again.

'Can't stand this heat,' Nora said, after a pause. 'I'm going hunting for refreshment. There's a fabulous little place a few streets away called Coffee Corner. They specialise in coffee and pastries, do nothing else, in fact. Ever been there?'

'Can't say I have, but it sounds as though I've missed something,' Cleone answered, thinking that if she went, she wouldn't have to keep looking at Ellis and his lady-love. 'All right, I'll come, Nora.'

She managed to catch Rick's eye and he mouthed the word 'Coming' over the heads of the other guests.

'Who's that Adonis you're communicating with?' Nora asked.

'He's my art editor. We're friendly.'

'Are you now? My, my, if he were *my* art editor, dear, we'd be more than just "friendly"!'

Rick sauntered over, put his arm across Cleone's shoulders and jerked her close. His grip was too strong for her to do much about it, and she began to regret that she had not tried harder to dissuade him from drinking so much.

She introduced him to the journalist and seeing the admiration in the woman's face, she looked up at Rick and realised just how good-looking he was. But her pulses remained obstinately regular and unhurried when he glanced down and caught her gaze.

'What's this?' he murmured. 'A mutual admiration society?' And he had put his lips to hers before she could guess his intention. As he lifted his head, she glanced nervously at Ellis. Of course he had to be watching them.

'My, my,' Nora said again, eyeing Cleone enviously, 'I know I'm a few years older than he is, but I wonder if he would do that to me if I gazed up at him like that?'

'Why don't you try?' Cleone asked, laughing in an attempt to release the tension inside her.

'Anything to oblige a lady,' Rick said, and brushed his lips over Nora's.

She turned pink with pleasure. 'Now I need that coffee to help me recover. Coming, you two?'

As Nora called 'goodbye' to her friends, Cleone's eyes went almost of their own volition to seek out Ellis. She wished she had kept them under better control, because if she had, she would have missed seeing Karin's radiant face laughing up at him as she slipped her hand into his. Not only did Ellis allow it to remain there, but to Cleone's jaundiced eyes his fingers actually seemed to tighten round Karin's and draw her nearer.

Watching them was agony and when Rick's hand took firm hold of her hand, she did not snatch it away. She allowed him to pull her to the door, but an odd feeling of guilt made her glance back to meet Ellis's watchful, critical eyes. She met his censure with a defiant smile, but the look he gave her in return was so derisive she wished she had resisted the temptation to provoke him.

In the brightness of the coffee house they settled down and talked.

'Have you been in the fashion game long, Cleone?' Nora asked, after they had ordered.

'No time at all, compared with you,' Cleone replied.

'I did hear,' Nora remarked, 'that *Salon* was in danger of folding up. Before your time, that was.'

Cleone sighed. 'And things haven't changed since I took over, so the danger's still there.'

'If anything,' Rick said, 'the circulation has gone down still more. Ben says that even the advertisers we did have are deserting us. I won't say anything about rats and sinking ships, but . . .'

'Well, if we do go down, it won't be for want of trying to reverse the process,' said Cleone. 'Mr. Firse and his—his confederates are about as sensitive to change as a rhinoceros.'

'Talk of the devil,' hissed Rick, 'and his accomplice, here they are. Who'd have thought the heiress and her aristocratic boy-friend would have lowered themselves to patronise this place!'

'But all the top people come here, Rick,' Nora told him. 'This place is famous for its wares. My word, though, she really is something, that woman. You've got to give him top marks for his taste.'

'Who said I didn't?' Rick answered, lost in admiration for the girl who was now moving her chair a few inches nearer to her companion's.

'You know,' Nora was saying, and Cleone was not sorry to have her attention diverted from the two across the room, 'I'd have said you, Cleone, weren't the type to stand up to the cut and thrust of our sort of work.' Nora studied her and dissected her features like an analyst in a laboratory. 'Eyes too bright and candid, expression too sweetly innocent, hair with its unruly little-girl curls . . .'

'And set against that,' Rick chimed in, stretching his arm ostentatiously across Cleone's shoulders, 'a figure which—er—shall we say, asks for trouble . . .?'

'That's her good luck,' Nora sighed, looking down at her own plumpness, 'but combine everything she's got and you're left with——'

'Dynamite,' Rick interrupted, bending down to kiss a cheek that moved away seconds too late.

Cleone wished he would stop flaunting an affection for her which he did not really feel. The coffee arrived and as they drank it, commenting favourably on its superior flavour and tang, Nora elaborated on her theme.

'I doubt if you're tough enough to stay the course, my dear. You know, if you were to be successful in widening the scope of that magazine you're editing, your work would be much harder, what with coping with promoters trying to get publicity for their goods, manufacturers being nice to you only for what they can get out of you in the way of space in your paper, and so on. It's not the glamorous life people seem to think it is.'

'Tell me, Nora,' said Rick, his arm still possessively lying across Cleone's shoulders, 'how much influence have you journalists got on the fashion you write about? Can you, for instance, "kill" a style stone dead at birth?'

'Probably, if we ever tried, Rick. But it's rare. We usually report what we see and leave it to the public to make up their minds. But contrariwise, a fashion writer who works for a daily newspaper can, if she wishes, help a fashion catch on simply by writing about it in glowing terms. If her timing is right, and her ability to select or reject a new style is good, and if she can see the fashions being shown to her in the context of the times, and—very important—put aside her own personal likes and dislikes in describing and recommending them, then she'll have the fashion world at her feet, begging for her attention.'

'So now you know,' Rick said, looking into Cleone's face and squeezing her shoulder, 'if you ever use your magnetic charm successfully on our Ellis over there, and manage to persuade him to bring *Salon* up to date, you know what's coming to you.'

'But according to Nora,' Cleone tried without success to remove herself from Rick's embrace, 'I'll be giving up soon, because I'm not the type to stick it out.'

'You make me sound like a fortune-teller, dear. I can't read your future.' She glanced across at Ellis and Karin. 'I'm willing to foretell theirs, though. I hear wedding bells for those two in the near future. Judging by the way they keep looking at each other, it won't be long, either.'

Cleone experienced an unpleasant feeling of revulsion, and she knew it was not caused by the over-warm atmosphere or the effects of the excellent coffee.

'Talking of the Firse family,' Nora went on, 'have you been invited to the François ball tonight?'

'Yes,' Cleone answered, 'but only because I'm one of their paid retainers, no other reason.' She stood up, preparing to leave. 'Rick's going to be my partner, aren't you, Rick?'

'Yes, and looking forward to it, darling.'

Nora raised her eyebrows at the endearment. 'Lucky you two. Have a good time.'

Cleone walked out into the cool air, leaving behind the chatter and laughter, and lifted her face, letting the rain-laden wind stroke her cheeks. She saw the greyness of the skies that held a downpour, heard the hurrying footsteps of the passers-by seeking shelter, felt on her skin the first stinging, astringent, neutral drops of rain, restoring her balance and her reason. She knew she had returned to the world of real things and had expelled from her lungs the brittle artificiality of the circles of high fashion.

She had seen Ellis with the girl who was so obviously his future wife and who fitted into his environment with perfection. By comparison she, Cleone Aston, was an alien, an onlooker, a passer-by.

She recalled the austere beauty of his flat and acknowledged that, however much she loved him, and even if he had ever come to love her in return, their worlds could never have met; that although their immediate presents might brush shoulders for a time in the course of their work, their pasts, their different social backgrounds would act as a divisive factor and send them separately into the future.

CHAPTER VIII

LATER, Cleone dressed for the dance without any expectations of enjoying herself. The flowing folds of the François evening gown rippled over her shoulders and down to her feet. Its incandescent colour enveloped her body like a tongue of flame, emphasising the paleness of her features.

But with the make-up she had applied and with the unusual brightness of her eyes belying the deep unhappiness which was battened down inside her, she seemed to have undergone a personality change which intrigued her. It worried her, too, because although others might take her to be the complete sophisticate she looked, she knew that inside the delectable wrapping with which she had covered herself, her essential simplicity remained untouched and the openness and absolute sincerity of her nature had not changed at all.

When Rick appeared in the doorway of her flat, he took a deep breath and bowed low. His eyes glinted with the anticipation of a child looking at a table spread for a party and he told her that, in the delicious outfit she was wearing, she would be lucky, as far as he was concerned, if she got through the evening unscathed.

She flung round her shoulders a black velvet cape she had borrowed from Sarah, and with mock solemnity allowed Rick to escort her to his car. He apologised for its lack of polish and the torn state of its upholstery, and said that if he had known in advance that he was partnering a member of the aristocracy, he would have brought his limousine.

The dance was being held at a large exclusive hotel near the François residence. Rick's arm was round her waist as they paused in the doorway for the announcement of their arrival. A few eyes turned casually their way, withdrew, only to swing back again, this time opened wide with astonishment. Most of the guests were professionals from the fashion world and there were few amongst them who would miss a François original.

Rick, delighted with the attention, played up gallantly. With a flourish he tucked Cleone's arm in his and they walked with slow dignity across the floor to a table for two. There was no sign of Ellis, but his father was there, surrounded by people—close friends and designer colleagues—all of whom formed an effective barrier between the man of the evening and his guests.

Cleone and Rick were having their third drink when there was a distraction at the entrance to the ballroom. The son of the designer had arrived. By his side was the department store heiress who had dropped her role of influential and sought-after buyer and had become instead a beautiful woman on the arm of the man she intended to marry. Their names were called and the crowd which swarmed around them cut them off from view.

Now he was there, but what of it? Cleone knew he would probably not even spare her a glance, let alone a word. The dancing had begun and Rick led her on to the floor. He held her close, commenting on the softness of her hair against his cheek, on the delicate touches of perfume on her skin and on the excellence of her dancing.

She smiled up at him, determined that he, at least, would enjoy the evening at whatever cost to herself. He seemed delighted by her gaiety and she knew he was thinking he had got the response he had been angling for for a long time.

Once she caught Ellis watching them, but she didn't care. If he could flaunt his lady-friend as though she were the most desirable creature in the world, then she could do the same with her escort. So she gazed raptly into Rick's eyes and it did not occur to her that she might be playing with fire.

Ellis rarely left Karin's side. They moved everywhere as a team, in perfect harmony. When he did leave her, it was for an occasional duty dance with a client of his father's.

A buffet supper was served and Rick fought his way through the crowd and collected two plates of food. Cleone ate with determination rather than appetite. Then Rick saw someone he knew and pointed them out with a nod of the head.

'D'you mind if I have a word with them?' He took her hand. 'Come with me, and I'll introduce you.'

'You go, Rick. I don't mind waiting here for you.'

So he left her with a smile and she wondered if she had lost him for the rest of the evening. Sighing with resignation, she drained her glass and looked around. The atmosphere was heavily laden with an unpleasant mixture of perfume and cigarette smoke. Cleone held her breath, rejecting it and feeling that it was choking her and corroding her lungs.

She was racked with a craving for fresh air and freedom like a man trapped in a sunken submarine. Her eyes lifted to the chandeliers, scintillating and brilliant overhead. They blurred into vagueness in the hazy, overheated atmosphere and as she stared, reality receded and they seemed to change for a piercing moment into sunlight sparkling through the leaves of a tree.

Reality encroached on her reverie and the illusion faded and died. Her vision cleared, she lowered her eyes and noticed idly that Maria was now the favoured one. She was in Ellis's arms and gazing up at him as raptly as all the others he had partnered.

She too was wearing a François gown and with her perfect figure, she revealed its beauty as only a trained model could. Then it was Annabelle's turn, and there was the same look in her eyes as Ellis took her round the floor.

Emilie, Ellis's mother, held court at the other end of the ballroom, looking elegantly bored and wearing one of her husband's creations. White, low-necked and graceful, it softened her usually querulous features into a rare beauty.

Cleone became conscious of Rick's prolonged absence and searched among the guests for a sight of him.

'Miss Aston?' She throbbed back to life at the sound of that voice. His arms were raised, inviting her to dance, and she went towards him as inevitably as a tributary joins a fast-flowing river. The lights were low, the music was a love song and the memories of the past which came crowding in became a torment.

He said, the words just reaching her ear, 'My father's dress suits you. Once it would not have done, but, as I predicted, your personality has altered to match its sophistication.'

She looked up, imploring him of all people to understand. 'Deep down I'm no different. Can't you see that?'

He merely smiled as if he knew better. After a while he asked, 'How is Ivor?'

'Well, thank you.'

'Have you seen him lately?'

'He's coming for the weekend.'

There was silence until he asked, 'When are you getting married?'

She shrugged. 'Soon, probably.' She added, trying to force a reaction from him, 'We may bring it forward.'

'Very wise.' That was all he said.

She drooped and his arms seemed to feel it and tightened to support her. But his hand on the bareness of her back was impersonal and cool like the hand of a passing acquaintance. Under the emotional impact of the music she closed her eyes and heard again the urgency and anguish in his voice that night he had made his passionate plea. She had loved him, she had needed him, but because she had listened to her pride, she had sent him away.

When she saw his exchange of smiles with Karin as they passed her with her partner, the pride that had triumphed that night whispered again that she had been right to reject him.

The music ended, but still he did not leave her. He sat her down, gave her a drink, sat beside her. Why? she asked herself. Then her brain tripped as she stumbled over the answer. *She was wearing a François gown.* Hadn't he commented on it? Now, for a time, she had her share of the son's undivided attention, the soft words, the smiles. It was like being picked out in the darkness by the headlamps of a car—anything in fact to draw attention to the François original she was wearing.

Rick was sitting alone now and frowning. He stood up and made his way unsteadily round the hall. He stood in front of her, put his hand on her wrist with a proprietorial gesture and jerked her up.

'Lost your way, partner?' he growled, obviously the worse for drink, and moved away, pulling her behind him.

Feeling she should apologise to Ellis, she looked back at him over her shoulder, but he was studying the tip of his cigarette as if he suspected it of containing explosives.

She said petulantly to Rick, 'You look like a snowcloud that's got mixed up with a heatwave. What's the matter?'

'Gone over to the enemy?' he muttered. '*I'm* your partner, not the great designer's son.'

They reached their table, but he pulled her past it. 'Come outside. I need some air.'

There was a balcony adjoining the ballroom and Cleone shivered in the chilly darkness. Rick sat on a bench and pulled her down. He kissed her so suddenly she had no chance to take evasive action.

He became possessed of an animal ferocity. At first she struggled, but recognising his greater strength gave up and lay passive and quiescent in his arms. She knew that circumstances would prevent him from going too far. She let him kiss and caress her, repugnant though it was, and hoped his passion would soon have run its course.

After a while she sensed that they were not alone. There was a movement nearby to confirm her suspicions and now she did try to break free. She managed to hold him off and saw, in the half-light, that Ellis Firse was watching them. As he turned away, she caught the look in his eyes. It expressed the deepest disgust she had ever seen on the face of a man. It came at her like a car out of control, wrecking her dignity and leaving her self-respect a write-off. Then he was gone.

She renewed her efforts to break away and this time, to her surprise, Rick let her go. He was holding his head.

'Good grief,' he muttered, 'if you use those tactics on every man who tries to get his way with you, you'll remain intact to the end of your days. What did you expect from me in that outfit,' he gestured towards her dress, 'brotherly love?'

'I'm sorry, Rick,' she said, her mouth dry, 'but I don't play that sort of game. I thought you knew.'

He made an impatient movement.

'If you want to shed me and find another partner,' she offered, feeling sorry for him now, 'then go ahead. I'll sit it out for the rest of the evening in a corner.'

She picked up her bag and went to the cloakroom. She renewed her make-up, combed her hair and wished the colour would come back to her cheeks.

When she returned to the ballroom she saw that Rick had taken her at her word. He had found an attractive girl—Cleone thought she must be a model—and was leading her on to the floor.

She stood in the doorway searching for sanctuary and found François' eyes on her. He moved towards her, his hand outstretched. His face was flushed, his eyes brighter than she had ever seen them. His animation, his near-joviality was completely out of character. The presentation of his collection was obviously like heady wine to him.

'Come over here, my dear. You look charming in my gown. Am I more in favour with you now because of it? You approve of *couture* at last?' He did not require an answer. He presented her to a crowd of strangers and they eyed her with reluctant interest, as though resenting being asked to admit a newcomer to their exclusive circle.

'Meet Miss Aston—a *couturier* in embryo.' He lifted the

hand he was holding. 'She has the "green fingers" of the true designer. Everything she makes with them—for herself, you understand, only for herself—is good.'

Ellis, standing near, raised a cigarette to his lips and his eyes, as they narrowed and came to rest on her, were full of insult and she coloured angrily. How could he stand in judgment on her like that when his own behaviour with the opposite sex would not stand examination?

Now his father appealed to him. 'My son will agree with me. Won't you, Ellis?' But his son merely flicked another look of contempt at the girl he was talking about and turned his head away. 'My son pretends to be impartial,' François laughed, 'but I know he is not.' The head remained averted.

Still François had not finished with her. 'I'll tell you a secret that not even Miss Aston knows. If she were to whisper the word, I would offer her an apprenticeship in my House.'

He watched her astonished reaction and saw the doubt and consequent recoil from the idea. 'But it wouldn't work, would it, my dear? You are, perhaps, my sternest critic.'

The words were familiar. Once, in happier times, the son had used them about her. Now the father...

'She is displeased with me,' François went on, 'because she maintains that I am so far behind the times that there will soon be no more François.' The other guests laughed. 'But we have a surprise for our young friend, haven't we, Ellis?' He raised his eyebrows at his son. 'Now?' he asked, and Ellis nodded, walking towards the platform. François followed.

The music was silenced. The announcement, when it came, brought a round of applause. François told them, in the hesitant tones of one who was unused to public speaking, that in the near future he would be opening a boutique and designing for the ready-to-wear market. When the clapping had died down, he went on,

'It is an idea which has been germinating in my head for a long time. It took a young whirlwind to come into my life,' he smiled at Cleone, 'and create the necessary climate to make the idea grow.'

He descended the short flight of steps and took Cleone's hand, putting it to his lips with a gesture that was partly gallant and partly an attempt to live up to the foreign image he had tried so hard to create.

He did not release Cleone's hand. Instead he offered it to his son, who walked away saying, 'Karin is calling me.' But Karin was deep in conversation with another man and was calling no one.

Nonplussed, François looked round, saw Antoine on the edge of the group and called him over. Antoine took the proffered hand with alacrity, drew Cleone on to the floor and she spent the rest of the evening with him.

He was good company, less intense than Rick and considerably less demanding. He asked where her partner was. She told him, with deliberate vagueness, that he was somewhere about and, with a laugh, that he seemed to have found greener pastures. Antoine looked into her face and read between the lines of her answer. Not to worry, he said reassuringly, he understood.

And she had good reason to appreciate that understanding of Antoine's as the evening passed, because every time her attention wandered from him to Ellis, which was pretty often, he did not seem to resent it. Once he followed her eyes, and Cleone wondered if he had guessed her secret.

Whenever Ellis was near, she found herself watching him. When she could not see him, she wondered where he was. What, she asked herself, did he think of her now? In her heart she knew the answer, but she did not care to face it.

When it was time to go, Rick came wandering back. He told her he would take her home, but Antoine tried to intervene.

'Cleone, my car is outside. If you like, I'll take you.'

She looked at Rick, and despite his semi-drunken state, thought she could manage him. She thanked Antoine but said she would go with Rick after all.

Ellis saw them leaving. Rick called out 'goodnight', but Cleone kept her eyes down. To have looked at him would have been asking to be hurt, like rubbing her knuckles deliberately against a brick wall.

In Rick's car she drew away from him. He laughed and said, 'You're quite safe now, dearie. I'd no more tackle you again tonight than I would a judo expert.'

If she hadn't been so tired, she would have laughed at the irony of the whole situation. There was Rick grumbling about her lack of co-operation, while Ellis held her in contempt for her 'permissiveness'.

Rick apologised next morning for his behaviour at the dance.

She smiled up at him. 'I've forgiven you. I took it from whence it came, if you understand me.'

He winced. 'That tells me exactly what you think of me.'

'Anyway,' she told him, 'I'm expecting my fiancé this evening. He's calling for me here, so you'd better keep out of his way, hadn't you, otherwise he might take it upon himself to defend my honour!'

Secretly, she was amused at the thought of Ivor defending anyone's honour. She had accepted long ago that after they were married she would have to fight life's battles for both of them.

She called them all into her office to tell them of François decision to go into the ready-to-wear market.

'Does that mean,' Sarah wanted to know, 'that it won't be long now before we get the go-ahead to alter the style of the magazine?'

'You could be right,' Cleone said thoughtfully. 'Shall I ask the powers-that-be himself?' Dare I phone him? she wondered. Yes, where the magazine was concerned, she would dare anything. After all, this was business, not a private matter.

Despite her attempt to reason away her fears, her pulse rate accelerated as she asked to speak to him.

As soon as he answered, she said, 'Mr. Firse,' she crossed her fingers and lifted them up to show the others, 'in view of your father's announcement last night, does that mean you'll soon be giving us permission to change——'

'The answer, Miss Aston, is *no*!' The receiver was slammed down.

She stared at her blotter. So he hadn't forgiven her. No one disturbed the sympathetic silence. She took out the editorial she had been forbidden to publish and contemplated it sadly.

'You're not using that, Cleone, are you, after what he said?' Ben asked. 'We love you too much to lose you!'

She sighed, gave him a sad smile, said, 'The temptation is overpowering,' and slipped it back into the drawer. 'It's so stupid, the way they keep burying their heads in the sand. Don't they realise that either they will have to change *Salon* or it goes out of circulation?'

When Ivor arrived, he knocked on her door timidly and put his head round it as if expecting an Alsatian dog to leap up and savage him. Cleone pulled him into the room and it was obvious that the girls admired his good looks, while his self-consciousness and uncertainty seemed to bring out their maternal instincts.

'He's sweet,' Joanna whispered in her ear.

In the lift going home, Cleone pushed her arm possessively into Ivor's. The lift stopped at the seventh floor and Ellis got in. He looked with interest at Ivor and Cleone had to introduce them. Ivor blushed when he heard who Ellis was, and Cleone wished fervently that he had more self-confidence so that she didn't have to act as a prop to him all the time.

Ellis tried to converse with Ivor, but soon gave up and seemed thankful when the lift arrived at the ground floor. He left them, wishing them a good weekend.

But for Cleone it was a bad weekend. As it progressed,

the likelihood of a marriage between them ever succeeding lessened with every hour they passed in each other's company. She had never spent so much time alone with Ivor before. At home, they had been together only for an afternoon or an evening.

When, on Sunday, she found herself longing for his departure, she knew it was time to think seriously about ending their friendship. Yes, she decided, that was all it was—a friendship. She had hoped that with Ivor loving her she would one day succeed in putting Ellis Firse out of her mind. But Ivor did not love her any more than she loved him.

She saw him on to the train with relief and felt that the kiss they exchanged was more in the nature of a farewell than a binding seal on their love.

Towards the end of the following week, Ellis walked into Cleone's office unannounced. He didn't ask if she was busy, he didn't apologise for interrupting, he didn't even say 'good morning'. He pulled up a chair opposite her and, with the desk between them, sat down.

She waited, hands clasped tightly on her lap, until he chose to begin. His long pause before starting seemed deliberate and she grew irritated, thinking of the work she had to do.

At last he said, inspecting his nails, 'You had a good weekend with your fiancé?'

'Yes, thank you.'

'You actually found something to talk to him about?' His tone expressed amused surprise. Annoyed, Cleone did not bother to reply. 'Tell me,' now he was fiddling with an envelope on her desk, 'is he always as difficult to converse with as he was when I met you both in the lift?'

She chose her words carefully in reply. 'He—doesn't always find it easy to communicate.'

'No, I thought not. So you'll spend the rest of your life coming to his rescue conversationally and filling in all the embarrassing gaps which his inarticulate nature creates.

Not to mention shielding him from the harshness of life, as you will obviously have to do.'

Did he have to be so right? 'That's my business,' she said, hoping her sharpness would bring the discussion to an end.

But he would not let it rest. 'Agreed. But, having met your homespun boy-friend, I begin to see why Rick Walsh, with his looks and his polish and his—er—persuasive technique, is making such headway with you.'

'I'm sorry to disappoint you,' she answered stiffly, 'and to have to rip open your pre-packaged ideas about my promiscuity, but we're friends, nothing else.'

'But of course,' he smiled sardonically, 'friends. I do understand what you mean.'

Incensed by his sneer, she remarked coldly, 'Don't judge my moral standards by your own. Anyway, I'm marrying Ivor.'

'Of course,' he said again, his voice smoothly cynical, 'you're marrying Ivor, the acquiescent, obedient, background boy-friend who doesn't intrude excessively into the important part of your life, and who is always there for you to produce like a revolver as a "hands off" warning to would-be violators of your chastity.' His eyelids drooped. 'As I well know.'

She stirred uneasily under his gaze, knowing he was too near the truth for her to retaliate effectively. Then, realising that her silence was in itself an admission of defeat, she looked up and asked,

'What did you want to see me about, Mr. Firse?'

Her business-like tone brought a mocking smile to his face. 'To ask you a favour, Miss Aston. I hasten to add,' he taunted, 'on behalf of my father, not myself. You allow yourself to confer favours on others—I can think of one in particular'—she knew he was referring to Rick—'but for some reason you exclude me from that category. However, I dare say I shall survive. You aren't the only female pebble on my beach.' She realised that her hands were mutilating each other. How insulting could he get?

'To return to the reason for my visit, you may recall that my father had an awkward client, a lady whose—er—statistics so nearly match your own? This client is living up to her name and is being very awkward about a number of outfits my father has designed and made for her. You know she rejected the dress which he passed on to you?' She nodded. 'Well, she's apparently threatening to do the same to the other things. My father thinks that if she saw these clothes on a model, saw them in action, as it were, on a living figure, she would appreciate their value and their effectiveness and agree to take them. Since he has no girl on his books with the required measurements, he is hoping you'll come to his rescue again and wear these clothes for this client to see.'

'Me—do modelling?' She shook her head. 'I'd be hopeless at it. You need months of training and instruction in grooming and so on to do that sort of thing. And I haven't got what it takes. I'm not sophisticated enough. Take my hair for a start.' She ran her hand over the curls which immediately sprang up again when the pressure of her hand had passed.

'I'm aware of the untameable nature of your hair, Miss Aston,' he said softly. 'I've looked at it often enough. Sometimes, when you goad me beyond endurance, I'd dearly love to take a handful and——' The pulling action of his hand effectively finished the sentence.

She said decisively, 'I'm sorry, the answer's "no". I'd probably lose him the sale, instead of clinching it.'

It was clear that he was going to get what he wanted. 'Miss Aston, that dress my father gave you—you agreed it was beautiful. It was also costly . . .'

'Putting me under a moral obligation, Mr. Firse? Blackmail, in fact?'

'Quite right, Miss Aston,' he agreed blandly. 'Blackmail.'

Now she was angry. 'I knew you'd want payment for that

dress. Just like those shoes—you never give anything without wanting something in return.'

'If I had—as you put it—wanted something in return, my sweet,' he turned the two words of endearment into an insult, 'there have been many occasions on which I could have taken it.'

She looked down. 'Please accept my apologies. I withdraw every word.' She looked up, her eyes heavy. 'When does he want me to do it?'

'Tonight?' She nodded. 'Eightish? Shall I call for you?'

'No, thank you. I'd prefer to make my own way there.'

He shrugged. 'There's also something else. More important, perhaps—to you. Tomorrow the board of management is meeting. I asked you some time back if you would be prepared to appear before them to support your case for an alteration in the style of the magazine. Well, tomorrow they're prepared to listen to your case. Could you get a few facts together and hold yourself ready at any time during the meeting to come down and—charm them into submission?'

She heard the sarcasm, but paid no attention to it because her thoughts had been plunged into a state of anarchy by his question. Somehow she restored them to order and felt herself in charge again. She faced the fact that now the time had come to fight for something she had wanted ever since she had taken up her job, she was quite unprepared. It would take hours to put down on paper all her arguments, hours she simply hadn't got. The afternoon was filled with engagements and the evening would have to be spent modelling for François.

'Well, what's the answer?'

She rose to his challenge. 'I'd be delighted to address the board of management tomorrow.'

'That's my girl,' he whispered, and went out.

François welcomed her like an old friend. He led her into the dressing room adjoining the *salon* and told her his client had not yet arrived. 'My son is picking them up.'

By 'them' Cleone assumed he also meant the client's husband.

'You do realise, Mr. Firse, that I've never done any modelling?'

'My dear Miss Aston, I don't expect anything of you except to stand before my client and let her see the clothes.' He looked at her face. 'If you would have no objection, I should like Vanda here to put a little make-up on you and perhaps,' he smiled, 'try to get a little order to your hair. But apart from that, all I want you to do is to wear the clothes as naturally as you wear your own.'

He left and Vanda came in. She obviously knew a lot about cosmetics. Under her attentions, Cleone watched her face change from youthful simplicity to youthful sophistication. 'This isn't me,' she protested silently, and closed her eyes against her own reflection.

Madame Hilaire, the senior *vendeuse,* appeared and hustled Cleone into the first outfit.

'The lady client is here,' she whispered.

'What's her name?' Cleone wanted to know.

'She's American,' Madame Hilaire replied. 'Her name is Mrs. Gabriell.'

'Does she know I'm not a real model?'

'She knows all about you, my dear.' Madame Hilaire gave the coat Cleone was wearing a loving pat here and there. 'A perfect fit,' she enthused. 'It might have been made for you.'

Cleone had to admire the dark brown coat with its fur-trimmed sleeves and collar. She wished she could achieve this perfection, this flowing line and impeccable fit in the clothes she made.

'Do I go in now?' she asked, a catch of anxiety in her voice. Suppose she let François down? Suppose the client went away empty-handed?

Madame Hilaire pushed her gently through the doorway and led her into the *salon.* François was there, his smile of encouragement beckoning her in. Beside him was his client, Mrs. Gabriell, and at her side sat another woman. As Cleone's eyes cleared, she recognised Karin Connar, looking captivating in black, her almond-shaped eyes narrowing a little as Cleone approached.

Cleone noticed with a shock how alike the two women were. They could have been sisters. She discovered, when the introductions were made, that they were indeed sisters.

She had expected that Ellis would be there. He was sitting at the back, his arms folded, his expression smug, as though he was fully prepared to enjoy the next half-hour. As she turned and turned again at Madame Hilaire's command, she wished him a mile away at that moment.

The next garment she modelled was a white, ankle-length evening gown, its material shot through with metal thread giving it a subtle silver hue. The neckline plunged deep, wide and daring, almost to the waist where a silver belt gave provocative emphasis to the wearer's shape.

She had never worn such a dress before, its extreme sophistication being entirely alien to her nature. She glanced uncertainly at Ellis to see how he was taking it and the subtle message in his eyes made her lower hers in confusion. She tried to dismiss him from her mind and to concentrate instead on smiling persuasively at the client who was, after all, the most important person there.

After that came a fur-lined ski outfit, followed by two day dresses and an elegantly tailored grey suit. Last of all she modelled a great swirling cape, deep red in colour and trimmed with white fur.

Then it was over. In the quiet of the dressing-room she flopped exhausted into a chair. As she dressed again in her own clothes, she heard the buzz of conversation in the next room. She was given coffee by Vanda and praised by Madame Hilaire. Then they left her alone.

Now there was silence from the *salon* and she assumed they had all gone. Reaction set in and she was stung momentarily to tears, feeling abandoned and unappreciated by those she had tried to please.

'I might as well go home,' she thought, and picked up her handbag.

There was a movement in the doorway and she looked round.

'Come and have a drink, Cleone.'

She followed Ellis into the empty *salon*. 'I thought you'd gone with the others,' she said.

'They haven't gone. We're in my parents' private apartments.' As they walked side by side he asked, 'Tired?'

'Very.'

'I'm not surprised. You did well. My father was pleased with you.'

'Did his client——?'

'Yes.' He smiled. 'She was most impressed with the clothes—and the girl wearing them.' He looked down at her. 'You've missed your vocation. You were born to model clothes, not to write about them. The only thing you lack is height.' His smile was intended to provoke. 'But you make up for that in other ways—persistence, for instance, and eloquence, not to mention downright impudence.'

She opened her mouth to retaliate, but they had arrived at his parents' sitting-room. François turned as they entered. He thanked Cleone, shook her hand, then put a glass into it. Nan Gabriell patted the seat beside her, inviting Cleone to sit down. She did not have her sister's faultless looks, but she had something else—warmth and liveliness which were as much a magnet as Karin's beauty.

'Did you like the new additions to my wardrobe, Miss Aston?' she asked. 'Did you feel good wearing them?'

Cleone knew that Ellis, standing beside his mother, would be listening and would take pleasure in using against her any praise she might give to the clothes, which were of course *couture*, pure and unadulterated.

Nevertheless she replied, 'I loved them, Mrs. Gabriell. I only wish I could achieve such perfection when I make my own things.' She glanced down at herself, realising too late how she had drawn attention to the suit she was wearing. She looked up and found Karin's eyes upon her, eyes which reflected her home-made image as surely as the great mirror which dominated the wall above the fireplace.

Defiantly she challenged the pity in those beautiful cold eyes, and with the same defiance stared at Ellis, but he was looking at Karin.

'You're very clever,' Mrs. Firse said in her lifeless way. 'It's rather ironic, but I hardly know how to push a needle through a piece of material. And as for cutting out a dress . . .'

'You sure haven't got to worry about that, Mrs. Firse,' Karin remarked, 'with a husband to provide all the clothes you need.'

Karin laughed up at Ellis and he smiled down at her.

'Where do you live, Miss Aston?' Nan Gabriell asked. 'In London?'

'I have a flat here,' Cleone told her, 'but my home is with my parents.'

'You don't mean to tell me you're not married? A sweet young girl like you . . .'

Cleone heard Ellis move and frowned up at him, catching the end of a grin.

'I have a—a boy-friend,' she told Nan Gabriell. 'We're planning to marry some time soon. We're saving up for a house.'

'Oh, how *sweet*!' came spontaneously from the heiress to her father's fortune.

Feeling reduced to the size and physique of a rag doll, Cleone stood up. The pages of notes she would have to make in preparation for her appearance in front of the committee the next morning were scratching at the back of her mind like a mouse under the floorboards.

'I'm sorry, Mr. Firse,' she said to François, 'but I really must go.'

'I'll take you back,' Ellis said.

'It doesn't matter, Mr. Firse——' But he was not listening.

François thanked her again and Mrs. Gabriell wished her happiness in her married life. 'We won't meet again,' she said. 'I'm off to the States in a few days to visit my parents.' She laughed. 'My husband—he's British, you know—has given me a month and says if I overstay my time, he will come and kidnap me!'

'Are you going with her, Karin?' Mrs. Firse asked.

Karin looked up at Ellis, apparently trying to gauge his reaction. 'It—er—depends,' she said.

Ellis did not respond. Instead, he followed Cleone out of the room.

'You needn't have bothered,' she told him coldly. 'There was no need for you to leave Miss Connar.'

He ignored the statement and led the way outside. It was dark and it was raining. She sank with deep relief into the luxury of Ellis's car. As they drove along she watched with a detached sort of interest how the raindrops hurled themselves with self-righteous fury against the windscreen, only to merge ineffectually with each other and run away in rivulets down the glass. The weather was in perfect accord with her mood. She couldn't have stood a starlit night.

'Well,' he asked, his tone spiked, 'I gather you enjoyed modelling *haute couture*, the real thing?' She detected a sneer in his voice as he put emphasis on the last words. 'Are you still determined to worship the shoddy, the artificial, the mass-produced—those sort of garments which you claim are representative of our times?'

'The description of the clothes is yours, not mine, and in any case it's totally wrong.' She sank back into her corner. She was not in the mood to fence with him. 'You're probably only saying it to annoy me.' She flirted with a shadow of suspicion. 'The object of the exercise tonight,' she said slowly, 'wasn't by any chance to brainwash me, was it? To let me get the feel of *couture* at first hand, to persuade me in a subtle sort of way that my attitude to it is misguided?'

'No, it was not,' he snapped, his baiting tone abandoned. 'My father asked you in good faith to do this favour for him for the benefit of a valued client. As he told you himself, he was delighted with you for doing it.'

She subsided into her corner again, ashamed.

'I don't think you realise,' he said, after a long silence, 'how—yes, I must say it—how privileged you are to be admitted into my father's private world. You must have some magic about you'—he said it as though he had never discovered such a quality in her—'which has made him let down his mental drawbridge and let you in. He pulled it up again pretty fast.' He said grimly, 'Not even my mother has passed his rigid test. As you may have noticed, she and I are hanging around on the other side, waiting, hoping some time to gain entry.'

Waiting. That was how she had thought of Ellis's mother the first time she had seen her. 'But I'm waiting, too,' she wanted to tell him, 'for the unattainable, for you, Ellis.' Then she remembered the way Karin had looked at him and knew that if she, Cleone Aston, did wait for Ellis Firse, she would have to wait all her life and longer.

'I suppose,' she said, reproaching herself even as she spoke the words, then changing her tone and trying to pass it off as a joke, 'now I've done some modelling I automatically qualify to be called "sweetie" and put on your list of girl-friends.' It came out unfortunately not as a joke, but as a challenge.

His laughter was loud and derisive and it provoked her to continue rashly, 'I also no doubt qualify to be given the brush-off whenever you don't feel like my company.'

He grinned malevolently. 'You could be right. Even to being given the final brush-off, the ultimate sanction—dismissal.'

That silenced her and they did not speak again until he drew up in the side road adjoining the block of flats where she lived. He looked at her speculatively in the light of the street lamp, then his hands closed over her arms and he pulled her round to face him.

'So you've put yourself on my list of girl-friends.'

'No, I haven't.' Her voice rose apprehensively and she tightened up, wishing his face was not in shadow so that she could read his expression. 'I meant it as a joke.'

'Did you now?' His tone was soft, insinuating. 'Well, joke or not, in my opinion it can mean only one thing—that it's where you really want to be. So,' his voice deepened as if in anticipation, 'we'll give you a taste of what it's like to be one of my girl-friends.' He lowered his head.

'I'm marrying Ivor,' she cried, twisting away from his lips. 'I'm marrying——'

He said, through his teeth, 'I didn't hear you say that to Rick Walsh on the night of my father's dance, when he was doing this to you ... and this ... and *this*!'

His kiss had begun before she could take a breath deep enough to see her through to the end of it. It was intimate, subtly insulting and, as she found to her dismay, irresistible. As the minutes passed, she felt herself yielding to him passionately and without restraint until it was quite beyond her power to withstand the demands he was making on her. She became wholly compliant and he could do whatever he chose with her from that moment on.

But unaccountably, he stopped. He stopped and raised his head. She could not see his eyes in the darkness, but his voice was harsh as he ground out, 'The next time you let a man get as near to you as this, *sweetie*, and he's not your husband, it won't be one atom of good imploring him to stop just because you're marrying someone called Ivor. Remember that the man almost certainly won't be a gentleman as I am—my God, I must be, otherwise I wouldn't just be sitting here talking!—that his physical strength will be greater than yours and that his power over you will be such that he could just take it—and you—from here.'

He bundled her over to her side of the car, got out, opened the door for her and did nothing to help as she stumbled through the rain towards the entrance to the block of flats and disappeared inside.

He had taken his revenge at last for what had happened on the night of the dance.

CHAPTER IX

CLEONE hardly slept that night. When she did, her dreams were haunted by the scene in the car. She was filled with foreboding when she entered her office next morning. Things would go against her—she was convinced of that.

She had not prepared a single note for her appearance before the board of management. She had been too distressed to put pencil to paper after leaving Ellis. She hoped that nothing important would crop up during the morning to prevent her from writing down a few ideas before being summoned to their august presence.

As the others came in to wish her luck, she told them she wanted to 'raid their brains' and that it was 'their ideas or their jobs'. They helped her as much as they could, but when she read the notes through afterwards they were in such disorder she could hardly follow them.

The call came sooner than she had expected. 'Would you please go down to the boardroom at once, Miss Aston,' Ellis's secretary said over the phone, adding in a cheerful whisper, 'Sooner you than me!'

As she sidled through the door of the long, narrow room, she had a blurred impression of masculinity of all shapes and ages, and at varying stages in the balding process. She was curtly told by the managing director to sit down. He seemed to be acting as chairman of the meeting.

A man with a kindly face and spectacles pulled up a chair for her near the end of the table and she tried to make herself as inconspicuous as possible while the discussion eddied about her head. Instead of listening, she surveyed the enemy front line with considerable apprehension.

There were gentlemen who could be described as 'worthy', others might just be called young. Some were formidable as they peered over their spectacles, others benign and grandfatherly. There seemed to be hundreds of men in that room. In fact, there were less than twenty.

Restive, still, her eyes roamed again and surprised her by focussing on a member of her own sex. In demeanour and shape, she was the essence of motherliness, but in everything else as forbidding as an ancient, impregnable fortress. Nearby sat a girl, perhaps a little older than Cleone herself, looking bright, vivacious and, compared with her companions, incredibly modern. She'll support me, Cleone told herself, clutching at any straw of hope with terrified fingers.

But in fact, all the bright young woman did during the whole of Cleone's interrogation was to put on a smile of encouragement and leave it there.

'Miss Aston!' The clipped tones of the managing director were a reprimand for her wandering attention. Cleone rose. The moment she had been waiting for had arrived.

As she stood there, trying to get her brain into working order, the deceptively motherly lady turned suspicious eyes upon her, regarding her with something akin to horror, as though she was suffering from a terrible disease called 'youth'.

'Never mind,' those eyes seemed to gloat, 'time will cure her of that, as it cures us all.'

So much, Cleone thought, for the advocacy of my own sex.

She sought Ellis's face, hoping to draw strength and support from him, but his expression as he stared at her from his exalted position at the head of the table was frightening in its blankness and formality.

As she held his gaze, she could think only of what had happened between them in the darkness of the car and she wanted to slide under that table and curl up with embarrassment.

He folded his arms and said in his most clipped executive tones, 'Will you begin, Miss Aston?'

Begin what? she wanted to say. Have I got to start from cold? No questions to help get me going, no guidance, just thrown in the lake and it's my own fault if I fail to surface? Her notes were shaking in her hand and it occurred to her that she was crushing them so badly they would soon be unreadable, so she loosened her hold on them and they fluttered to the floor.

The kindly gentleman beside her dived under the table and picked up the scattered pieces of paper one by one. There came an ominous sigh from the well-built lady, who was now looking as motherly as a prison wardress.

Ellis said again, and now there was impatience in his tone, 'Begin, Miss Aston.'

So Miss Aston began, in a voice that was so tremulous and so timid that some of the gentlemen put their hands to their ears.

'Speak up, Miss Aston,' the prison wardress ordered, so Cleone raised her voice and its resonance surprised even herself.

'What I'm asking for,' she plunged straight in, her eyes fixed firmly on her crumpled notes, 'is for more freedom in determining the design, style and content of the magazine *Salon*. I should also like to be empowered to alter its name.' A hum ran round the room like the buzz of a swarm of thwarted bees. It occurred to her then to look for François, but she was relieved to discover that he was absent.

'My colleagues and I,' she went on, her voice gaining strength and conviction, 'consider that the name *Fashion Talk* would be more appropriate for these times, and would help to create the new image we are striving for.' There was no response from her audience. Somehow she must rouse them from their indifference.

'Fashion,' she said, approaching the subject from another angle, and hoping the bomb she was throwing amongst them would go off, 'must reflect the times.' She glanced round, noting the merest suggestion of a response to her words. She decided to continue her challenge, and enlarge upon it.

'*Couture*, in my opinion belongs to a time gone by, to a world of glamour and romance—and even those two words have a touch of the past about them.' This clearly offended some of her listeners.

'*Couture*,' she persisted, 'is part of history now.' The faces round her were beginning to register shock. She was bringing them to life at last.

'*Couture*,' she grew expansive in her imagery, 'reminds me of those rich landscaped gardens attached to great houses, which the public are allowed to walk in but can never own, can never feel the joy of saying, 'This belongs to me.' In the same way, you can look at beautiful *couture* garments, even be allowed to touch them if you're lucky, but own them? Never, unless you're approaching millionaire status, which most of us are not.'

A shocked titter ran round the assembled company, and Ellis's voice broke in smoothly,

'What you're saying, is it not, Miss Aston, is that *couture* is just a dream?'

'I suppose so,' she answered, wondering where the question was leading.

'And would you deprive people of their dreams?' She was still puzzled and showed it. He went on, 'Dreams, as I see it, are a necessary part of life. Even the psychologists tell us that. You surely agree?'

'I—suppose so.'

'To a woman, say a hard-working housewife, a mother of small, demanding children, a beautiful dress is a dream, is it not?'

His smug tone goaded her into crying, from the depths of her heart, 'What's the use of a dream if it's beyond reach? It can only tantalise and torment and in the end, even drive you crazy.'

She acknowledged silently that it was not really *couture*

she was talking about at all. It was her own secret dream of Ellis.

Her heart was throbbing now, but it did not inhibit her flow of words. Nor did the managing director's raised eyebrows. 'These women you're talking about—the sort of women I should like to have as readers of my magazine—if they saw a photograph of a *couture* dress and then saw its price, its incredible price—they'd throw the magazine across the room in disgust as if they'd been cheated. Then they would go to their nearest department store and buy a dress off the rack. It would probably last a season and then they'd probably throw it out. Next season, because of the speed with which fashion changes nowadays, they would buy another dress. That's how they keep up with the constant fluctuation in styles. You can have your dreams, Mr. Firse,' she cried, seeking Ellis's eyes and blinking back the moisture which was gathering ominously under her lids, 'they're no use to me.'

Ellis was frowning down at the paper in front of him and appeared to be doodling on it with concentrated ferocity.

'Nowadays,' Cleone went on, abandoning her notes altogether, 'designers—young ones who are in touch with life as it's lived today—are doing wonderful things with fabrics. They're putting materials together which once people would never have dreamed of combining—velvet with gaberdine, satin with tweed and so on. A woman can look different each day if she chooses. Once women—ordinary women—used to spend most of their lives longing to be able to clothe themselves in dreams—the sort that Mr. Firse has just been talking about. Now they're much more realistic, and practical too. They go out and buy the image of themselves they most want to present to the world. Mass-produced it may be, but in such quantities that it gives them great freedom of choice. You see, there's no room in life these days for the conspicuous extravagance of work done by hand as it is in *couture*.'

'Miss Aston.' Cleone frowned, mistrusting Ellis's baiting

tone. 'May I ask whether that outfit you're wearing is your own creation?'

She looked down at her pale blue suit. 'Yes. Why?'

'And you take pride in wearing it, because you made it with your own hands and because it's entirely your brain-child, created from your own original idea?'

What was he leading up to? 'I suppose so, yes.'

He pounced, his words as efficient in their destructiveness as a tiger's teeth. 'And you have the audacity to decry *haute couture*? You make your own clothes to a design which you have conceived in your own mind, and which you admit you are proud to wear because of their originality, yet you are trying to deny other women, without your ability, the right to wear clothes which have been designed and made especially for them by established *couturiers* who do what you do only on a much higher level? Why one law for them and another for you?'

She should have known he was trying to trap her!

'You're misrepresenting my case,' she came back at him, 'because you happen to know about my love of dressmaking. You're dragging it in, irrelevant though it is, for your own purposes.'

A shocked murmur rippled round the table and even the bright young woman looked a little disapproving.

'If you would consider what I have said with reason and calm, Miss Aston, you would see that it is quite relevant.'

'Anyway,' she said, changing course in an effort to ignore the grain of truth she had to admit was present in his words, 'we're not supposed to be discussing whether or not I approve of *haute couture*——'

'You introduced the subject,' Ellis interrupted calmly.

'I had to,' she snapped, 'because it was necessary to put *couture* into a proper perspective in order to support my contention that a change in policy where *Salon* is concerned is essential.'

She looked pleadingly round the table. 'What I'm asking is whether I'm going to be allowed to give *Salon* the kiss of life it needs or let it perish because of a standstill policy which is forced on me and prevents me from adopting the new approach which is vital to its continued existence.'

She took a deep breath and made a last desperate appeal. 'You must surely agree with me that you have to be on the side of progress in this world, this rat race we live in, otherwise you might as well give up, die and bury yourself in your own grave.'

She stopped. The impetus of her rhetoric had run out on her. There was a long, heavy silence, and she asked faintly, 'Is that all?'

Ellis raised his eyebrows and glanced round at his fellow board members. They nodded.

'Yes, thank you, Miss Aston.'

'That's all,' she thought as she closed the door behind her, 'and that's the end of me.'

A few days later, Sarah rushed into Cleone's office waving a newspaper.

'It's out,' she shouted. 'They know who makes the François lace.'

'*No!*' Cleone nearly choked with fright. She paled and groped for a chair. She read through the item Sarah thrust in front of her. The headline, at the top of the fashion column, shrieked at her.

'Source of François lace revealed.' The article went on, 'Now we know. An old lady, sitting in a lonely two-hundred-years-old cottage, makes the superb lace that trims *couturier* François' gowns. Her eyes are dim, her hands are worn and gnarled with age. But never mind, she turns out the most sought-after, the most exquisite lace in the country. Until the other day, it was the best-kept secret of the fashion scene. Now the whole world knows...'

The professional part of her mind still ticking over, she shrank from the journalese, the sensational treatment which the writer had given it. Then reality broke through and with it horror at how much she herself was to blame for betraying the secret. There was only one thing she could do now and that was little enough. She would have to apologise, and the sooner the better.

She thanked Sarah for pointing it out and dismissed her with a smile. Then she dialled Ellis's secretary.

No, Mr. Firse was not there, Carol said. He had been called away urgently. No, she did not know when he would be back.

Was it her imagination, Cleone wondered, or was that voice, usually so pleasant, just a little cooler this morning? She rang off and held her head. Of course she knew where Ellis had gone—to his grandmother's. He would be needed there to act as guard-dog, to keep the howling press from the door.

Then she thought of his father—she would phone his father. She must explain the position to someone in the Firse family.

She dialled the number and got through to the housekeeper. She gave her name and was asked to wait. A few minutes later, the housekeeper's voice said, 'I'm sorry, Miss Aston, Monsieur François is not available.'

'When will he be back?' Cleone asked, desperate now.

'I'm afraid I don't know.' When Cleone appeared to be persisting, the cold measured voice said, 'I regret I am unable to help you,' and the phone went dead.

Cleone refused to admit defeat. She would call at the François residence. The stout matronly lady who opened the door to her, and who seemed to be the housekeeper, asked her name and told her to wait. Nothing happened for some time.

The great hall where the fashion show had been held seemed enigmatic now with a secret silence. Had she been forgotten? No, the housekeeper descended the sweeping staircase, taking each tread with deliberate care, and came to a standstill a few feet away.

'Monsieur François is not available. I'm sorry.'

'But please, I would only keep him a few minutes . . .'

'Monsieur François does not wish to see you, Miss Aston.'

Cleone's control snapped. 'But I wish to see him!' she shouted, and moved as if to circle round the woman and make for the stairs. But the woman moved, too.

Incensed at such treatment, Cleone became stubborn. 'I'm prepared to wait,' she said, 'until Monsieur François consents to see me,' and sat on a chair.

The housekeeper gave an exasperated sigh and swept up the stairs again. A few moments later, François himself came down them, his face stiff and mask-like, his eyes stone cold.

'Mr. Firse,' Cleone appealed to him at once, 'I've come to say how terribly sorry I am about what has happened and to explain...'

'No explanation will undo the damage you have done, Miss Aston.'

'But at least I should like to tell you that it was not really my doing, that it was sheer bad luck that the particular journalist who saw the lace on my dress should recognise it...'

'I'm sorry, Miss Aston, I am not prepared to listen to any explanations, however plausible you may make them sound.' He half turned towards the stairs. 'The real victim in this unfortunate episode is my mother. She is the one you should have thought of before you blurted out your secret——'

'Mr. Firse, please believe me,' there were tears in her eyes now, 'I did *not* tell the journalist about your mother——'

But François had bowed dismissively and was walking away.

Now she had it, like a cold cruel wave breaking high over the promenade, and it was dragging her helplessly over the edge and into the sea. If she did not get out of that atmosphere, away from the rebuke in that rigid retreating back, she would submerge and drown.

'Shut out,' she thought, as she walked away from the

François residence for the last time, 'just as I used to be when he first knew me. He's gone back inside his castle, pulled up the drawbridge and left me on the other side.'

It was three days before Ellis returned. She knew when he was back because his secretary rang her. 'Mr. Firse wishes to see you at once, Miss Aston.'

There was no mistaking the coldness in that voice now. His secretary, because of her position, had, partisan-like, made his cause her own. If Miss Aston was an enemy of the man she worked for, then Miss Aston was her enemy, too.

So Miss Aston, like a captured guerrilla, went before the court to be tried. She stood before him, hands clasped behind her back, and the questioning began.

'I suppose you know why I've sent for you? I suppose you know where I've been? At my grandmother's cottage, fighting off packs of baying hounds who called themselves the press and who had come, it seemed, from all over the northern hemisphere. Now do you see what your little act of spite has done?'

'Spite, Mr. Firse?' Her bewilderment was lost on him.

'Yes, the cunning way you found of having your own back on me for not giving you your own way with the magazine.'

'But—but you're quite wrong. What happened was an unfortunate accident. A journalist sitting next to me recognised the lace. She——'

He was not listening. 'My grandmother asked me to spare you. But I said why should I? It was a miserable act of revenge.'

She shook her head and tried to speak.

'She disagreed, however. She said that what you did was only natural. Any young woman, any journalist with such a secret would be tempted to tell the world. She said, with incredible generosity of spirit on her part, that she couldn't blame you.'

Now the tears swamped her eyes. 'You mean your grandmother thinks I did it deliberately—even *she* does? But how could I? I love your grandmother. She's a wonderful woman. I wouldn't do that to her!'

He was silent, apparently prepared to let her go on. But his expression said clearly that his mind was closed on the subject.

'Surely *you* believe me, Mr. Firse? Once you said—you said you always got the truth from me...'

'Once, Miss Aston, I had a lot of illusions about you. I haven't got them now.'

'At least listen to the truth, even if you're not prepared to believe it.' She told him in detail what had happened at the showing of his father's collection. He heard her out, but made no comment.

'I must go and see your grandmother,' said Cleone, her voice urgent.

'You will not!'

'You can't stop me.'

'Oh, but I can. Before I left I gave strict instructions to my grandmother and the woman who is looking after her to refuse to let you in.'

She grew defiant. 'And if I do get in to see her, I suppose you'll use the ultimate weapon—you'll sack me.'

'I might even do that. The subject of your dismissal is never far from my mind.'

'You brought me here, Mr. Firse.' Her voice rose. 'On your own admission, you enticed me out of the surroundings I loved, out of the job I loved. Your "protégée", you called me. One of your discoveries.' She went on bitterly, 'Now I'm one of your failures, perhaps the only one. An error of your judgment. A mistake and, as such, a danger to your reputation as a connoisseur of women, so the sooner I'm out of the way the better.' She stopped. She had run out of ammunition. She waited for the return fire, for the retaliation, the sentence to be passed, but it did not come.

She turned towards the door, then she stopped. There

was something she had to know. 'Mr. Firse?'

'Yes, Miss Aston?' His voice was edged with weariness, like a long-suffering parent dutifully answering his child.

'Is it possible,' she asked hesitantly, 'for you to tell me what decision the board of management came to after I went out?'

He leaned back. 'Concerning what?'

His deliberate obtuseness nettled her and her rigid control slipped. 'You know very well what I'm talking about!'

He raised an eyebrow. 'I do, do I? If you're talking about your heart-rending appeal regarding the magazine, there was no decision. Even if there had been, I doubt if it would have gone in your favour.'

'No, of course it wouldn't!' she cried, angered beyond endurance by his casual attitude to a subject that meant so much to her. 'You made sure of that, didn't you, with your infuriating questions, and the way you tricked me into saying things I would never have dreamed of saying without your provocation.' Her failure to stir him to anger incensed her even more. 'How you can accuse me of spite and revenge when you were guilty of them against me at the board meeting——'

'I protest,' he said mildly. 'I was merely doing my duty as a shareholder. In any case, I knew exactly what I was doing in questioning you like that. And tell me, what have I got to be spiteful about where you're concerned?'

'You know very well you've never forgiven me for what happened—or what you thought happened—between Rick and me on the night of your father's dance. Though why you should take it upon yourself to be concerned about the way I behave with the men in my life is beyond me.'

He did not deny the accusation. He merely looked at his watch with a sort of tired patience and said, 'I'm very busy, Miss Aston...'

She slammed the door behind her.

It took Cleone only a few days to make up her mind. Then

she called an editorial conference to announce her decision. Her colleagues gathered round her. Rick half reclined as usual with his feet on the desk, Ben leaned against the windowsill and Joanna and Sarah shared the visitor's chair.

Cleone sat, her elbows resting on her blotter, her chin in her hands, looking utterly dejected. In sympathy, they all looked miserable, too.

'I'm going to do something,' she told them, 'after which heads—or a head—will roll. It will probably be mine. But I want to know, before I do it, if I've got your support.'

They waited, their faces betraying that they knew already what she was going to say. 'You know what I mean? That editorial—I've decided to use it.'

'But don't you remember what Mr. Firse said, Cleone?' Joanna asked, frowning.

'Joanna,' Cleone sighed, 'I've read the signs. I'm on my way out. Mr. Firse as good as said so the other day. So, if I'm going, it will be in a blaze of glory and for a worthwhile cause.'

Rick said, agreeing with her, 'Personally, I think that Firse junior—and by now probably Firse senior—have such a down on our editor here,' he nodded at Cleone, 'that whatever she does from now on is wrong. Almost anything will tip the balance and out she'll go.'

Cleone looked at them, one by one. 'I'll be willing to take the risk if I know you're with me and will support me to the bitter end.'

'We're with you all the way,' they assured her.

When they had gone, she took out the editorial, subbed it and sent it off to be included in the next edition of *Salon.*

'And that,' she thought, 'is the end of a beautiful career as a fashion editor. Short but'—she closed her eyes as the memories crowded in—'sweet, very sweet.'

She continued going the rounds of fashion shows and wholesalers, visiting boutiques and accessory manufacturers, living from one day to the next like a man who had been given only a few weeks to live. Her work had become all the more enjoyable now that there was so little time left.

She made the most of it, attending cocktail parties with Sarah, visiting photographic studios with Rick and dealing with accessories saleswomen who tried to talk her into giving them free publicity in *Salon*. Now and then she would remind herself, 'Not much longer now,' and feel a stab of regret, like someone who had given something away and immediately wanted it back.

The summons came sooner than she had expected. The issue of *Salon* which contained the forbidden editorial was not even out when the phone call came that 'Miss Aston was wanted by Mr. Firse.'

'This is it,' she thought, 'the beginning of the end.'

CHAPTER X

CLEONE had not seen Ellis for some time. She thought she could detect a change in him, but it was too elusive to pin down. His gaze settled on her for a few seconds, then moved away. She wondered if she looked as tired as she felt. It was a weariness which had come about with waiting for an end that was too long delayed, a waiting that had taken her to the limits of an anxiety which had dominated her thoughts day and night without respite.

Now that she was facing it, it was almost a relief.

He said, without preamble, 'That editorial you showed me some time ago—did you use it?' There was a light in his eye which reminded her of a lawyer cross-examining a witness, and who knew the answer he expected to get would assist him immeasurably in the furtherance of his case. In fact, he knew he had caught her at last.

'Yes, Mr. Firse.'

'In *Salon*?' She nodded, mistrusting his mild tone.

'And when will this particular issue be out?'

'In a few days, Mr. Firse.' Why didn't he pronounce the sentence, why was he dallying with her like a hunter giving his prey a run for its money?

'In spite of what I said?' She nodded again. 'In spite of knowing the consequences—your dismissal?'

'In spite of that.'

He looked down. 'Then there's no more for me to say.'

'But, Mr. Firse, I thought that with the coming change in the nature of your father's *couture* business, you might see your way to allowing me . . .'

He repeated, slowly and clearly, 'There is no more to be said, Miss Aston.'

She held her head high. 'A month's notice, isn't it, Mr. Firse?'

'Yes, you have a month in which to find another job.'

She returned to her office.

Some time later, Sarah found her crying. She pulled up a chair and put her arms round her neck. Rick came in, but Sarah sent him out.

After a while, the sobs grew less and Cleone apologised. Drying her eyes, she said, 'It's so silly to cry. I knew it was coming and I thought I was ready for it. But I wasn't.'

When Sarah heard what had happened, she grew indignant. 'We'll do something, Cleone. We don't want you to go. I'll see what the others suggest.'

She went out and a little later Cleone heard a noise that sounded like a general exodus from the ninth floor. She wondered if they had staged a walk-out, but knew they would not have done so without telling her first.

After about twenty minutes, she heard them return. As Sarah walked in, the phone rang. Miss Aston was wanted again by Mr. Firse.

'What now?' asked Cleone wearily.

'Sorry, love,' said Sarah. 'It's probably about us. We went to see him and tried to make him change his mind. We all had our say, Rick most of all, but I think Rick made things worse. Mr. Firse seemed to harden after that, although a bit earlier I'm sure he was softening.'

Cleone sighed. 'Thanks for trying, Sarah. It was very good of you all, but——' She shook her head and went down in the lift.

He seemed angry when she went in and she sank into a chair without invitation. She thought she could take just a little more sitting than she could standing. Her head was throbbing, her eyes puffed with crying. As she raised her head and looked fully at him, he took a breath to speak and stopped abruptly. But it was only a moment's hesitation.

He said nastily, 'A touching little deputation that was you sent me.'

'*I* sent you?' She was bewildered. 'It was their decision to see you, not mine. I knew nothing about it.'

'You expect me to believe that, when it was your boy-friend who spoke the loudest and longest in your defence?'

She frowned. 'My boy-friend? You mean Rick?' She sounded resigned. 'I suppose you're referring yet again to the night of the dance.' She shook her head. 'Ask Antoine about that. You won't believe me if I tell you what really happened. But it was good of Rick to speak out, it was good of them all. But I didn't send them.' Her voice wavered. 'In any case, I could have told them in advance that it wouldn't do any good.'

She could see he still did not believe her, and insisted quietly, 'It's the truth, Mr. Firse.'

He raised his eyebrows with studied scepticism and this goaded her out of her apathy. 'I always tell the truth. I always have.' She whispered, 'Especially to you.' Still he seemed unmoved. 'Why don't you believe me?' she cried, her voice shrill in its supplication. 'Why do you hate me so much that your judgment is warped where I'm concerned?' He moved restlessly to the window and stared out. 'What have I done to make you change towards me like this?'

Somehow she would make him look at her. She said, her spirit returning, 'Why should I send a deputation to you to plead for me? I wouldn't have this job back now, with you as an employer, not even if you trebled—or even quadrupled my salary.' He swung round to face her. 'You,' she shouted, 'you're not even human. *And that's the truth!*'

She rushed out, went up to her office, gathered her belongings together and went home.

In the days following the publication of *Salon*, Cleone's phone rang incessantly. It seemed as though the entire fashion world had read her editorial and was scenting a change.

She parried most of the questions, stalling in her replies, giving the professional, tight-lipped 'no comment' if pressed too hard. Then the advertisers began. They hadn't used the magazine before to publicise their wares, they said, because of its limited appeal and small circulation, but if there was a policy change in the offing...

She didn't get excited at the interest her editorial had aroused. She merely put all the calls through to the managing director.

'Let him cope,' she thought petulantly, 'it's not my worry any more.'

The internal phone rang. 'Yes?' she answered wearily.

'Miss Aston.' She tightened at once, recognising the curt tones. 'I'm getting one call after another from flaming advertisers mumbling something incomprehensible about policy changes and your perishing editorial. Who the hell's putting them through to me?'

She sighed. 'I am, Mr. Firse.'

'Then will you damned well stop!'

'If you wish, Mr. Firse. Who would you like me to put them through to instead—the chairman, your father?'

There was a noise like a roll of thunder in her ear.

'Never mind, Mr. Firse,' she said, her tone pacifying, 'it won't be much longer now, then I'll be gone.'

She replaced the receiver and burst into tears. But she couldn't allow herself to cry for long. She was going home for the weekend and could not arrive on her parents' doorstep swollen-eyed and tear-stained.

It was the end of the afternoon. Her coat was on, her suitcase in her hand. She looked round her office. One more week and then it would belong to someone else—her successor. The phone rang. She answered it automatically.

'Miss Aston?' came the familiar voice.

Anger burst out of her like lava from a volcano. 'No, it is *not* Miss Aston. She isn't here. I don't know who you are and what's more, I don't care! You can be the whole board of management as far as I'm concerned. Miss Aston's going home—and I mean home. In fact, she's already gone!'

She slammed down the receiver and rushed out to the lift. When it reached the ground floor, she fretted until the doors opened, then she scurried along the corridor, past a man who was standing in his doorway, staring at her as though she was a dangerous animal escaping from a zoo.

He made a pouncing movement as if to capture her, realised he was too late and retreated into his office. Painted on his door in large letters were the words, 'Managing Director'.

It was hardly a triumphant homecoming. She had to tell her parents she had failed. Worse than that, she had been ignominiously sacked.

Her father rubbed his hands and chortled 'I told you so' all the evening. Her mother nearly wept with chagrin because she would no longer be able to boast to her friends about the glamorous life her daughter was leading in London.

She did not enjoy her meeting with Ivor the next day. She had to tell him that although she liked him as a person, she had discovered that she did not love him. She was sorry, she said, because she had enjoyed their friendship.

She felt, illogically, that she had failed there, too, but knew in her heart that she did not want a marriage in which she would have had to bear all the burdens of decision-making. It was really Ivor's personality which was the root cause of things going wrong between them. She had hoped that, given time, he would have 'grown up'. Now she knew he never would.

He reacted much as she had expected. He said he was sorry, because he liked her very much, but if that was how she felt—he had shrugged—then there was nothing they could do about it. They parted friends.

That afternoon, Cleone dressed in the clothes she used to wear—her well-worn blue slacks, pink blouse and sandals—and wandered through the woods. She was going to visit Ellis's grandmother. She did not know whether she would be allowed to go in, in view of the grandson's instructions, but she was going to have a darned good try.

In fact, she had no trouble at all. Her knock was answered by a raised, inviting voice and she opened the door and walked in.

Mrs. Firse was in her usual seat, her hands busy with the crochet for which she had became famous. The sight of it gave Cleone a shock, but she exchanged smile for smile as the old lady drew her down excitedly to kiss her.

'I didn't know whether you'd see me,' Cleone said, sitting on the stool at Mrs. Firse's feet.

'My dear Cleone, why ever not? You mean because of my grandson? My goodness, I don't listen to him! He can't select my visitors for me, even though he thinks he can.'

'Mrs. Firse,' Cleone fiddled with the braid trimming on the armchair, 'I've really come to say I'm sorry.' She looked up into puzzled eyes. 'About the lace. Please believe me when I say that I didn't tell anyone the secret. It was just foolishness on my part for wearing the dress with your lace on it at the fashion show that day. I didn't think anyone would recognise it, although I should have known . . .'

'Don't go on, my dear. Of course I never believed you did it deliberately.'

'But you told Ellis . . .'

'Whatever I said that day I said to humour him. He was so angry with you it hurt me to hear him. How he could ever have doubted your integrity . . .'

Cleone's face began to crumple and she covered it with her hands.

'My dear child——' A hand came out. 'Don't cry.' But Cleone could not stop. She had been holding back the tears for so long, they came of their own accord.

'Is it Ellis?' Mrs. Firse asked softly. Cleone nodded. 'You love him?' She nodded again. 'And he loves you, so what's the trouble?'

Cleone's head came up at that and she shook it violently.

'But he does, my dear. He's loved you from the first day he met you.'

Cleone, still unable to speak for sobbing, stared at her.

'How do I know? Well, you remember he brought you here that evening?'

'Yes,' Cleone managed at last.

'You remember how excited I was?'

'Yes, but I thought it was because someone had come to see you.'

'Partly that, yes. But you see, a long time ago Ellis had made me a promise that as soon as he met the girl he wanted to marry, he would bring her to see me. He brought you.' She patted Cleone's hand. 'He's never, ever, brought any other girl.'

Cleone's spirits began to rise like the sun at dawn, but memories of the bitter animosity which now existed between them turned that dawn to dusk. 'Even if he loved me then,' she said, 'he doesn't now. I know he doesn't. He's grown to hate me so much, he's—he's even thrown me out of my job.' She stared at the carpet. 'In a way, I asked for it. I disobeyed his instructions. I thought it was for the best and in the interests of the magazine, and I hoped he'd understand, but——' She shook her head.

Mrs. Firse frowned, doubt clouding her eyes. 'I don't know, my child, I don't know. Somehow you must find out before it's too late.'

'But, Mrs. Firse,' she looked up, her eyes full of misery, 'it wouldn't work even if—if things did come right.'

Mrs. Firse looked puzzled.

'It's his way of life, it's not my way at all. I've seen his flat.' She shut her eyes, trying to visualise it. 'It's all so unreal it frightens me. It's so—so theatrical, like living all the time on a stage. I just wouldn't fit in at all.'

'I know what you're talking about, my dear. I felt the same when I went there once. But all it needs is warmth—a woman's touch to bring it to life. It needs to be lived in, and loved in, and made a little untidy. Then it would become a home. I'll tell you something—he has a tyrant of a housekeeper. She won't have a thing out of place. If he drops an envelope on the floor, she tuts and is after it like a dog after a bone!'

They laughed. Then Cleone sighed, knowing that the hopes Ellis's grandmother had raised in her were false, because Ellis loved no one. He might pretend, in certain circumstances, that he did just to get what he wanted and then, afterwards...

'There was a night,' she whispered, 'when he—when he——' She could not go on and shook her head helplessly. 'I sent him away.' She stopped again and the large antique clock on the mantelshelf ticked away the silent seconds.

She raised her eyes to the old lady's and said as if in self-defence, 'He's got so many women friends, Mrs. Firse, I couldn't see how, if he didn't love them, he could possibly love me.' She was silent. 'And I believe,' she went on slowly, 'that there has to be love between a man and a woman before—before...' She floundered again and felt a hand on her head.

'I do understand exactly what you are trying to say, my child.'

Another silence, then, 'But, my dear, you would surely not expect him to have lived the life of a saint—a young man, a bachelor, with his high executive position, his means, his good looks, to have turned his back on women? No, my dear. You could not expect it.'

'You make me feel so selfish,' Cleone whispered.

'No, only young. And time will remedy that.' Cleone rose. 'My only advice is this,' Mrs. Firse went on. 'You rejected him once. Knowing my grandson, he won't risk a second rejection. You will have to find your own way back to him.'

Cleone knew she must go. She did not want to tire the old lady by staying too long. She bent down to kiss the soft wrinkled cheek and two hands came up and held her face.

'Goodbye, my dear. You will come to see me again, whatever happens?' Cleone promised that she would. 'And no more tears, mind.'

With an effort, Cleone smiled, kissed her again and went on her way.

She walked barefoot across the fields and along the path which dropped down into the woods. She found her favourite tree and sat beneath it, her back against its trunk. She wondered how, in the space of one short week, she could ever get near enough to Ellis to follow his grandmother's advice. The barriers she would have to surmount were daunting.

There were the embargoes imposed by the administrative jungle they worked in, there was protocol to be observed and status to be considered, not to mention the fact that he wouldn't allow her within a mile of him anyway, because he hated the sight of her.

It was no good even thinking about it, she decided, taking off her sandal again and emptying out the pieces of dead leaves that had accumulated there. The difficulties were insurmountable.

There was a crunch of twigs and a rustle of bushes and she knew she was not alone. Someone was coming. When he stood there looking down at her, saying nothing, she was so stunned she forgot to breathe.

Then she saw his face. It was so lifeless, so devoid of any spark of human warmth that he might have been a wax impression of himself.

'*Ellis!*' The word jerked out without any help from her.

'Hallo, Cleone,' he said casually, as though he was accustomed to meeting her every day under a tree in the woods.

There was a long silence. 'I—I didn't know you were coming here this weekend,' she ventured at last.

'It was a last-minute decision.'

He was speaking slowly as if he were having to force himself to talk to her. His barriers were up and he had placed her firmly on the other side, as his father had done. Her hopes were dying for want of nourishment and there was nothing about him which suggested that he was prepared to satisfy their needs.

Words came into her mind, but she could not get them to form themselves into an orderly sequence.

He stood there, hands in pockets, huddled up as if it were the depths of winter, despite the fact that the sun was beating down and the birds were full of the joys of a late summer afternoon.

It seemed he was determined to give her no help. 'Tell him now,' said a voice like the whisper of the breeze. 'He's there in front of you. No doors, no desks, no lifts, no protocol to stop you.'

She shrank from the thought. She slipped on her sandal and he watched the action, his face still devoid of expression.

Then she stood up, and nearly sank down again. He looked even more formidable at close quarters than he did from the ground.

Her throat felt like a dried-up river bed. 'Ellis,' she croaked, 'Rick...'

He soon disposed of that. 'I know about Rick. I asked Antoine, as you suggested. He told me what he thought had happened. I'll accept his word. Forgive me for misjudging you.'

At least he had peeled off one layer of protective clothing, but what was left was enough to intimidate the boldest spirit, and Cleone's spirits were anything but bold at that moment.

If only her body would stop throbbing, if only she could calm herself and think more clearly about what to do next . . .

He reached for a cigarette and searched with apparent difficulty for his lighter. He showed every sign of preparing to move on and leave her. Desperately she thought of something to keep him there.

'Only one more week for me, Ellis.'

'Yes.' He was frowning because for some reason his lighter would not ignite. In the end he gave up and put the cigarette away. 'No doubt you've come home to prepare for your wedding.'

That was her cue. 'Now,' said the voice, 'tell him now, this minute, there isn't going to be a wedding.' But her pride chipped in, 'Suppose he rejects you, think of the shame.' But she had listened to her pride once before. Now she put it resolutely and finally behind her.

If he wanted her, she was his for the taking. If not, then she would go on her way saddened beyond words, but with no self-reproach for not having tried.

She told herself she was prepared for anything—for the embarrassed frown, for the cold withdrawal, for the brush-off he gave to all his girl-friends when they became too demanding.

She took a few steps towards him. One of her hands she slipped into his pocket and closed her fingers over his. The other she lifted and with it pulled down his head. Into his ear she whispered,

'It's not Ivor I love, Ellis. It's you.'

She felt his body stiffen, but he made no move. So she had gambled and lost. Blindly she turned and walked away.

She had been prepared for anything, she told herself, even this.

But she wasn't prepared for the way his arms came about her and stopped her in her tracks. She wasn't prepared for the force he used to pull her round to face him, or for the desperation with which his mouth sought hers and caught it and held it for minutes on end.

And she wasn't prepared for the way she found herself clinging to him as a man clings to a mast in a tumultuous sea, lest he be swept overboard and lost...

They were lying beneath a tree, Cleone's tree. She was looking up at the sky through the stirring leaves. He was looking at her.

'How did you know where to find me, Ellis?'

'I asked my grandmother as soon as I arrived. I knew you would be calling on her—defying my instructions again,' he growled, grabbing a handful of her hair, 'and I hoped to catch you. You'd just gone, but she told me where she thought I might find you, because of the way you were dressed—just as you were the day I met you,' he murmured against her lips.

'Yes, you see, darling,' she took delight in reminding him, 'I haven't changed as you kept insisting I would. The essential "me" is still the same.'

'My sweet, in saying that I was only voicing my deepest fears. I was terrified that the girl I loved would change into the sort of woman I had around me morning, afternoon and sometimes well into the evening. I didn't see how you could escape contamination from those you had to mix with. When I saw you that night with Rick I thought the change of character had taken place. All my vices took over—jealousy, pride, an irrational desire to get my own back. You had rejected me because you declared you were going to marry Ivor, yet you took on Rick, as I saw it, with open arms. Can you wonder that I was so angry with you!'

'That night at my flat, Ellis——?'

'That night I was going to tell you I wanted to marry you.'

There was a poignant silence. Then, 'Is that what you meant when you gave that mysterious answer to your grandmother's message?'

'Yes. Why do you think I spent the entire day with you after my return? Because after five weeks away from you—I should really have stayed on in the States to bring Karin back with me—I couldn't bear to let you out of my sight.'

'Was I—your "urgent business"?'

'You were.'

'And I had married you off to Karin!'

'I know you had, like a lot of people. But she was about as desirable to me as an immaculately dressed shop window dummy. What you didn't seem to understand—nor apparently did anyone else—was that I had to go out of my way to be nice to her because with all those potential orders she brought with her from the States in her capacity as buyer, she was one of my father's most valuable customers.'

'She was after you, you know,' she teased.

'I did know. My sweet, I wasn't blind to her—or any woman's—aspirations.'

'Only mine!'

'Yes, ironically, only yours.'

'Why did you phone me yesterday afternoon just as I was leaving?'

'You,' his hands settled playfully on her throat, 'were a little minx running out on me like that. I was going to do two things. One, offer you a lift home and two, give you your job back.'

She couldn't take that lying down, so she tried to sit up, but he wouldn't let her. 'You stay right where you are,' he ordered. 'I can keep you under control better that way.'

He took a little time to demonstrate the fact in unmistakable terms, then she came up for air, gasping, 'So I've won?'

'Yes, you little torment, you've won.'

'And I'm reinstated?'

'My darling, I can't sack my wife, can I?'

'But you didn't know then that I was going to be, so why the change of heart?'

'Because I'd just got the go-ahead for the new format of the magazine. I'd been fighting like hell for your ideas behind the scenes for weeks. The break-through came when my father made his decision—which incidentally was precipitated by the impudent intervention of a firebrand of a young woman called Cleone Aston—about going into the ready-to-wear market.'

'And I kept pestering you, didn't I, thinking it was you who were dragging your feet when all the time you were on my side...'

'You certainly were a little pest. And small thanks I got for the success of my efforts—a spate of rudeness in my ear over the telephone and the cold shoulder by a human tornado who looked as though she had just got a message that the earth was about to stop rotating!'

'I'm sorry, darling,' she whispered.

'I should think you are,' he said, accepting the kiss of apology she offered with very good grace indeed.

'Will your parents like me, Cleone?' he asked, with a trace of anxiety that endeared him to her even more.

'How could they fail? Anyway,' she added, with mischief in her eyes, 'once they see the size of your car, you're in!'

'Joking apart, I think we should go and see them.'

'Well, if you're old-fashioned enough to want to ask my father for his daughter's hand...'

'It's one of the rules I've formulated as I've gone through life—always be polite to the parents of the girl you're going to marry!'

'And how many girls,' she asked indignantly, 'have you been "going to marry"?'

'To be honest,' he whispered, his lips against hers, 'one. You.'

Later, he hauled her up and they walked to Cleone's home.

On the way, she told him, 'I'm wearing the sandal I threw at you.'

He looked down at her feet. 'Cherish it, sweetheart, then when we're married, we can preserve it for ever in a glass case, and when the kids are old enough to understand, we can point to it and tell them, "That's what began it all!"'

Mrs. Aston was in the kitchen when they arrived, and nearly dropped the iron she was holding when Cleone introduced Ellis.

Mr. Aston came from the dining-room, newspaper in hand, to see what was going on. The printed pages fluttered to the floor as he tried to take in what had happened.

He looked round the room as if suddenly conscious of its size in relation to what this man his daughter had suddenly produced as her fiancé would be used to.

'It's—er—a bit cramped in here,' he said, 'so come into the dining-room.' He saw that the table was still covered by the cloth and hastily changed his mind. 'Er—no, in here,' he led the way into the sitting-room. 'It's more—er—comfortable.'

Cleone had never known her father so ill at ease. With his kind of jaunty self-confidence he usually adjusted quickly to any situation, but this time he seemed floored.

Cleone and Ellis shared the couch, while Mr. Aston looked down on them like a man watching a time-bomb and wondering when it would go off. He saw his daughter slip her arm into the young man's and he thought with a rather naïve astonishment that, in so doing, she was linking herself—and in a roundabout sort of way her parents—to a considerable bank balance.

He saw her doing it with a 'now laugh at this one' look on her face and instead of slapping her down for being so cheeky, as he had often done in the past, he wanted to throw his arms round her neck and kiss her for being so clever.

'We're getting married, Dad,' she said, to which he replied,

'Er—yes, so I see. Congratulations.'

Ellis stood as Mrs. Aston came in, rolling up her apron and slipping it under a cushion. She had heard her daughter's announcement and, in a daze, kissed her on both cheeks.

When Ellis bent down, an inviting smile on his face, for her to do the same to him, she stood on tiptoe and kissed him like a little girl who had been told to be nice to a rich uncle.

They all relaxed after that, and talked over a cup of tea. Cleone was sure her mother was sitting there making a mental list of her friends, deciding in which order of priority to phone them and boast about the fabulous—and wealthy—son-in-law she was going to have!

It did not seem to occur to Cleone's parents to ask about Ivor. It was so obvious that he had fallen by the wayside, knocked off his motorbike, as it were, by this man in the large and costly car it seemed he owned, that they didn't even bother to mention Ivor's name.

'When is the—er—wedding going to—er—take place?' Mr. Aston wanted to know, still hesitant and still plainly suffering from shock.

Ellis looked at Cleone. 'I have to go to the United States again in ten days' time, and I want to take her with me,' he said, and there was no mistaking the decision in his voice.

Now it was Cleone's turn to suffer from shock. 'But, darling——' she breathed.

Ellis kissed her upturned mouth. 'I'll give you a week,' he told her, smiling. 'Then we'll have three days to get used to each other before we go.'

Cleone thought that if they stayed much longer she would have to take measures to revive her parents from their stupor—and include herself in the treatment!

They waved to her mother and father all the way down the street, and Cleone felt as if she was going away for a month. When they were out of sight Ellis said,

'Now to make my report back to my grandmother. She gave me strict instructions, if I found you, to go and tell her exactly what happened between us.'

'It'll be a report without words,' Cleone laughed. 'One look at us and . . .'

He kissed her regardless of interested onlookers and whispered, 'This will be a repeat performance, darling. I took you there once before, but this time it will be a true homecoming.'

They knocked and went in. Two eyes, full of hope, searched their faces. A voice, tremulous with emotion, asked, as it had the last time, 'Ellis?'

He nodded. 'Yes, Grandmother. This time it's the real thing.'

Two hands, shaking a little, stretched out, drawing them towards her.

The Mills & Boon Rose is the Rose of Romance

Every month there are ten new titles to choose from — ten new stories about people falling in love, people you want to read about, people in exciting, far-away places. Choose Mills & Boon. It's your way of relaxing.

August's titles are:

A WILDER SHORE *by Daphne Clair*
Elise had married Shard at last, and they should both have been blissfully happy – so just what was going wrong with their marriage?

MASTER OF ULURU *by Helen Bianchin*
On a working holiday in Australia, Jamie found herself encountering the forceful Logan more often than was good for her peace of mind.

BETRAYAL IN BALI *by Sally Wentworth*
Gael's happiness seemed complete when Leo Kane married her and took her off to Bali – but then he set about carrying out his revenge on her . . .

THE SILKEN BOND *by Flora Kidd*
Lyn loved Joel Morgan, but what chance would their marriage have when it would always be haunted by the ghost of Joel's lovely dead wife Sabrina?

THE CHALLENGE *by Kerry Allyne*
Debra thought herself lucky when she was offered a job on a cattle station – but that was before she met the exacting owner, Saxon McAllister.

MAN OF POWER *by Mary Wibberley*
It was to keep him out of the clutches of a designing woman that Morgan Haldane had asked Sara to pretend to be his fiancée – at least, that was his story . . .

DESERT DREAM *by Rosemary Carter*
The only way Corey could get herself on to Fraser Mallory's expedition was to disguise herself as a man – but she didn't remain undetected for long!

LOVE BEYOND REASON *by Karen van der Zee*
What had gone wrong with Amy's happy and promising love affair with Vic Hoyt? He had completely changed and was now bitter and hostile towards her.

OBSESSION *by Charlotte Lamb*
Nicola had no intention of being just another scalp on womaniser Lang Hyland's belt. But would she have the strength of mind to stick to her guns?

THE SILVER FALCON *by Yvonne Whittal*
After six years' separation, Tricia had met Kyle Hammond again – and knew that all those years had not killed her love for him.